WHEN THE LAST PETAL FALLS

A Robeson Family Novel

CHRISTINE MICHELLE

About the Book

Bea:
Till death do us part...

That was how it was supposed to go.
We didn't even make it that far.
The day of my wedding, I found out that Law, the man I
planned to marry, didn't really love me. Maybe he did, just
not enough.

Watching a petal fall from my bouquet, almost like a silent
tear commemorating the end of a relationship, instead of
the beginning of a blessed partnership, felt like a sign.

Then, my best friend, Ky, stepped in.
He told me that all was well and to meet him at the altar, as
planned.

I took a leap of faith, and hoped that Law would be there
waiting for me.

He wasn't there.
That didn't stop me from getting married though.

The difficulty came when Law realized his mistake a moment too late, the moment when I pledged myself to someone else.

KY:

Stepping in to be my best friend's replacement husband was the best decision I ever made. I'd been in love with her since we were young, and I wouldn't miss out on the opportunity to finally make her understand how I felt.

Author's Notes

For those of you who read The Forgotten Wife – It is important that you remember this: Bea's story takes place before Mina's.

Sometimes, the muse speaks when she's not supposed to. While writing When the Last Petal Falls, I had an idea for Mina's story, and as it sometimes happens, I only came up from that idea to sleep. A week later, I had the first draft of Mina's book finished. I don't know what kind of magic takes place when those things happen, but the book just bleeds out of me and I have to oblige.

Mina's book was supposed to be the final installment of the Robeson Family Novels and it ended up releasing first.

Chronologically, the order for the siblings HEAs is:

When the Last petal Falls

A Different Husband

The Forgotten Wife

Enjoy!

Chapter One

BEA

My reflection was a liar.

Maybe everyone felt that way on their wedding day, then again, it might just be me. Either way, something felt off, and I couldn't put my finger on what it was.

The dress was stunning, highlighting all my best features while hiding away my imperfections. I had left my hair mostly down, in a tamed version of my natural curls. The sides were pinned back with gorgeous flowers so none of it could escape into my face and obstruct my view of the ceremony - of my soon-to-be husband.

Even my makeup was perfect.

"What the hell is wrong with me?"

There was no one left in the room to answer the question since I'd sent them out so I could breathe for a minute in peace without someone fussing around me. Every little primp and fluff from my well-meaning mother and sister nearly sent me over the edge. Everything annoyed me and I didn't think that was how I was supposed to feel on my wedding day.

More worrisome was the giant boulder in the pit of my stomach that felt as though it was crushing my very soul. There was something about the day, the wedding, my soon-to-be husband, or maybe it was just me, that screamed that I shouldn't be doing this. I'd had this feeling a few times throughout my life and it had never been wrong. My father asked if I had cold feet, my mother argued that I did not, my sister seemed far away and lost in her head as usual, and my brother – no one knew where he was.

As I stared at the vision of the perfect bride that they'd turned me into, my hands shook. Law had felt distant lately, but I thought it was just pre-wedding stuff getting in the way.

"What if it wasn't?" I whispered to my reflection.

They say you're only crazy if you answer back when you talk to yourself. Luckily, my reflection simply stared back into my eyes, probably wondering why I wasn't enjoying the fact that I looked like a damn princess for the day. Then again...

"What if I'm the one making a mistake?" I questioned my reflection. I clasped my hands together to stop the way they shook and chastised myself. "No, I can't think like that on my wedding day."

It wasn't only my wedding day when those thoughts crossed my mind though. I'd been wondering if this was all a mistake for weeks – okay months really. I loved Law, but there was something missing. Someone missing was more like it. My best friend had also grown distant the closer got to the wedding. Maybe that was all it was. This wasn't wedding day jitters, it was a fear of losing my best friend freakout.

I took a deep breath and tried to shake off the negative thoughts about Ky. There had been moments in my life where I crushed on him and wished he would see me as more than just a friend. There were plenty of times when dreams played out in my fantasies of me walking down the aisle to meet his smiling face, dancing until dawn, and stuffing cake in one another's faces. Once I was older, there were the occasional naughty honeymoon fantasies too. Despite my crush, we had only ever been best friends. If you looked up unrequited in the dictionary, there was more than likely a picture of me staring at my best friend who never noticed.

I'd given up on having anything beyond friendship with Ky after I started dating Law. The one thing I was never willing to sacrifice was my friendship with him. I'd even had fights with my fiancé because he didn't want me spending as much time with Ky, even when my best friend had one of his girlfriends along. I had put my foot down, and everything went back to semi-normal, considering Ky only ever tolerated Law. At least, I thought everything had gone back to normal. Law loved me. I loved him. Ky would always be my friend.

"Then why have they both been so distant lately?" I asked myself. Truthfully, I wasn't sure which man in that scenario upset me more.

A knock at the door startled me out of my thoughts. I opened it to find my fiancé's best man, Todd Bainbridge standing there. Todd grinned at me and then slipped a note free of the inner pocket of his tux jacket.

"You look stunning, Bea."

"Thanks, T." The words were a whisper as the paper landed between my fingers. "What is this?"

His shoulder bounced up and down as the man stared down at my hand where the paper now rested. "Figured it was something to do with your vows, or his. Law didn't tell me, just said to deliver this to you and to be nice." He winked at me then. "Guess he didn't want me hitting on his hot fiancee and stealing you away on his wedding day."

I rolled my eyes at the man because he might have been my husband's - soon-to-be husband's - best man, but he was a dog of the worst sort. Honestly, that was an insult to dogs everywhere. I wouldn't be surprised to find him trying to hump someone's leg as I walked down the aisle.

"Was that all?" I asked when he continued to stand there and stare.

"Did I mention that you're beautiful?" His question threw me because I honestly didn't think Todd liked me. "I mean, truly gorgeous, Bea. I don't know why I ever allowed Law to make the first move."

What in the hell was I supposed to say to that? *Thanks? I guess I was ugly all the other days you saw me.* Todd was an idiot, and I had no clue what he meant about Law making the first move, since my fiancé's best man barely spoke to me the day the three of us met.

"Sorry," he pointed over his shoulder. "I guess I better get back out there so the show can go on."

I nodded my head and waited for the dimwit to back up, so I could shut the door again. The note in my hand demanded all my attention. Maybe it would be the reassurance I needed. This letter would reassure me that here was nothing to worry about, and walking down the aisle to marry Law was the right thing to do.

Bea,

I've written this letter to you exactly twenty-two times. That's how many it has taken, not to get it right, but to gather the courage to make sure you read it.

We are about to get married.

We are supposed to get married, and I shouldn't have to keep reminding myself of that.

The thing is, I can't wait at the end of the aisle for you to show up. It wouldn't be fair to either of us when I feel the way I do. I love you, don't ever doubt that. The thing is, I've been the one having doubts lately. I never cheated on you, but I don't think I'm ready to settle down yet.

There is someone else who caught my eye. If we were meant to marry, and I was meant to be with only you for the rest of my life, then how would that be possible? She didn't just catch my eye, Bea. I guess, that's what I'm really trying to say here. I am enamored with this woman, and I would regret never taking the chance to follow my feelings. I don't want to end up being that man – the one who marries out of duty – even if there is love there too – and then cheats on his wife because he can't get his mind off someone else. That wouldn't be fair to anyone involved.

I'm sorry that I didn't come to this conclusion earlier.

I'm sorry that I've disappointed you.

I'm sorry, Bea.

I wish I had been a better man for you.

Love,

Law

My dress suddenly felt three sizes too tight as I tried to get air to move in and out of my lungs the way it was supposed to. The whooshing sound in my ears was all I could hear, and yet my body refused to produce a single tear. It was like I was stuck in some sort of emotional limbo where a weird, calm sort of panic took over and held me in stasis.

"Bea!" I managed to turn in time to see my best friend, Ky, rushing toward me. "What's going on?" I couldn't find my voice and instead handed the note off to him. "Where did you get this?"

"Todd."

He nodded and then I watched as his eyes scanned the paper. His lips thinned, pulling tight against his teeth as he read, and I could see as a fine tremor started in his hands. The movement made the edges of the paper sway.

"Right." He said as he took a deep breath, then seeming to have decided something he turned his eyes down to me then closed them completely. Those long, dark lashes of his fanned out across his cheeks for a minute before he opened them again and pointedly stared into my own.

"I want you to forget his letter," he said while shaking the paper. "Get your butt down that aisle in five minutes. I promise you that everything will be okay."

"But-" I started to argue as I snatched the letter from him, to hold it up as proof that there was no need for me to take that walk and humiliate myself in front of all the guests who had gathered.

"No. You listen to me; this is Todd's idea of a fucking joke. I want you to march your butt down that aisle. I'll be waiting."

"Okay," I agreed, though I had no clue why I would. The note was no joke. I knew that because I knew Law's handwriting like I knew my own.

"Okay?" It was a question. Ky wanted reassurance that I wasn't going to go back on my word.

"Promise. I'll humiliate myself for you, if that's what you want."

He rolled his eyes. "I'd never purposely allow you to humiliate yourself and you know it."

"What about that time-"?

His eyebrows arched up toward his hairline. "That was a one-off," he informed me, but there was no hiding the chuckle as he relived the memory. When I glared, he cleared his throat nervously and took a step back before bending forward once more and placing a sweet kiss to my cheek. "Five minutes, Bea! Any longer and I'm coming to get you."

After Ky left the room, I watched the clock. As the minutes ticked by, I began to sweat. Then my legs started to shake. Was I really going to walk down that aisle knowing that my fiancé wouldn't be there waiting to marry me? Oh, my word! Why did I agree to Ky's demands? Why couldn't I just back out?

I trusted him.

That single thought worked to calm me. It was true. I trusted my best friend like no one else on the planet. He was my person. The one I could rely on. He would fix this. Knowing him, he went to beat the shit out of Law and force him to wait for me down the aisle and then he'd have us taken straight to a marriage counselor after our vows were spoken. Law would see that what he was really feeling was pre-wedding jitters, not the fact that he was falling for someone else.

I could already breathe easier. I was sure that was exactly what Ky would do. So, when the minute hand ticked off the fifth one since Ky marched out of the room, I turned the knob and met my father in the hallway. He seemed nervous as he wiped his brow with a hanky before he tucked it back into his pocket.

"Are you ready for this?" He asked, and there was something off about his tone that put me back on edge.

"Of course. Ky said everything was going to be okay, and I believe him." Granted, I wasn't sure if Ky took the time to fill my father in about the letter, but there was no time to explain. Instead, my father tucked my arm in his, turned us toward the open doors that led to the man I was about to marry. At least, that was how it was supposed to happen. I wasn't normally superstitious, but I found myself crossing my fingers as we took our first step into my new future.

Chapter Two

LAW

"I NEED you to take this to Bea." Todd stared dubiously at the paper I thrust into his hand.

"What is this?" His eyes narrowed on me. He suspected something was up, but I also knew that Todd would never read the letter. He would dutifully deliver it to Bea and then come back to stand up as my best man. I should tell him. He was my best friend, and by giving him the letter to deliver, he would be the messenger who had to deal with the aftermath.

I should have just marched into the church and sent everyone home. It was the right thing to do to tell everyone that it was all my fault, and that I couldn't marry Bea. Not today. Maybe not ever.

She was the wrong woman for me, or at least that's what my gut had been telling me for the past month. I should have told everyone, but there was somewhere else I needed to be. Instead, my best friend was going to be the one to deliver the news.

I couldn't tell any of them though, not even my best

friend. There was a reason that I was about to hightail it out of there, and truthfully, I didn't want anyone to stop me. Besides, if Jackie rejected me, I'd come right back here and marry Bea. I'd tell her the letter was a joke and blame it on Todd. I'd marry her if the woman I was interested in refused me. Yeah, I was a dick. Still, it was better to go find out than to wonder, or to cheat later, right?

"Just make sure she gets it before it's time for her to walk, but only just before. Leave it to the last minute, otherwise you'll ruin the surprise." Maybe 'surprise' was the wrong thing to say, but I hoped that things would turn out with Jackie, and if not, I needed a buffer of time to be able to get back and marry Bea.

I sound like such a dick.

Todd reached out and wrapped his hand around my lower arm as I turned to leave. "Where in the hell are you going?"

"I'll be back," I quietly reassured him, though I couldn't turn around and say it to his face. I think we both knew I might be lying. He dropped his hold on me and laughed.

"You're a fucking prick for doing this." I sighed, because what could I say? He wasn't wrong. "If you don't make it back in time, I might steal your woman. Todd had coveted my relationship with Bea from the very beginning. He had seen her first and demanded we stop to help the woman who was stranded on the side of the road. I had argued against stopping until she stood up and flashed a hopeful smile our way as Todd slowed down. In another completely dickish move, I beat him to the punch when I asked her out. All's fair in love and friendship, right?

"If you think you can," I challenged him. Todd only

laughed again and then walked out to the lobby. Eventually, he would listen and go deliver the message to my fiancé that I wouldn't be waiting for her when she walked down the aisle.

If Bea didn't think Todd was a disgusting horn-dog, I might have to worry that he'd keep to his word and steal my girl. He wasn't really that bad, but I might have exaggerated a bit about his lively hit 'em and quit 'em sex life to keep her from falling for his charms when we first started dating, and then I just never stopped.

Yeah, I was definitely a dick!

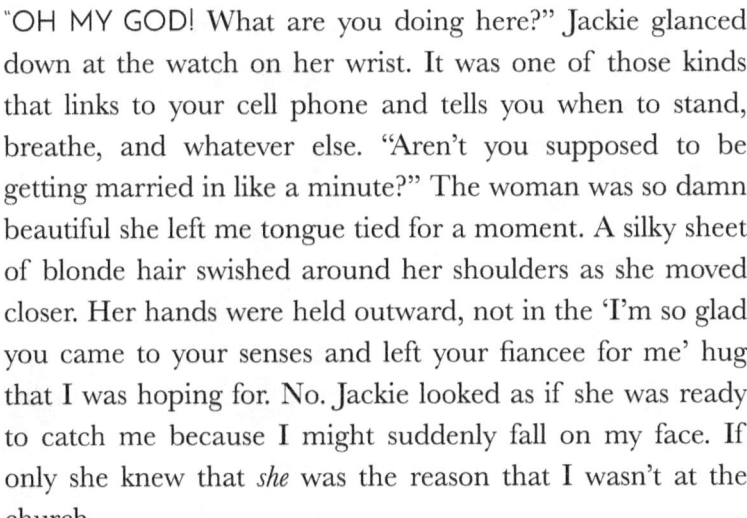

"OH MY GOD! What are you doing here?" Jackie glanced down at the watch on her wrist. It was one of those kinds that links to your cell phone and tells you when to stand, breathe, and whatever else. "Aren't you supposed to be getting married in like a minute?" The woman was so damn beautiful she left me tongue tied for a moment. A silky sheet of blonde hair swished around her shoulders as she moved closer. Her hands were held outward, not in the 'I'm so glad you came to your senses and left your fiancee for me' hug that I was hoping for. No. Jackie looked as if she was ready to catch me because I might suddenly fall on my face. If only she knew that *she* was the reason that I wasn't at the church.

"I couldn't do it." My words sounded desperate as I said them. Her bright blue eyes widened almost comically as the gorgeous woman stood there waiting on my explanation. Before she could recover from the shock of what I'd just said, I took hold of her still outstretched hands and pulled her into me. It was a connection with her that I needed before explaining myself. Just in case.

"I couldn't do it because there's something here." I stepped back and gestured with my hands indicating the two of us.

"What?" That one word came out as more of a startled gasp than a clear question.

"I've been falling for you," I admitted. "Ever since we worked together on the Carlton Project, you are pretty much all I can think about."

"No," Jackie whispered and took a giant step away from me. "Bea is my friend."

I nodded, knowing that to be true. The girls had met at a work function I'd escorted Bea to, and they got along so well that my fiancee ended up spending more time with Jackie that night than she did by my side. I was busy schmoozing clients most of the night, but still, it hadn't gone unnoticed by anyone.

"This is just cold feet talking. It's natural." Jackie tried to tell me. I shook my head to deny her words. She was wrong and I think we both knew it. The way she nervously chewed on the bottom of her lip as her chest heaved from her labored breaths told me she felt the same, even if she didn't want to admit to it.

"It's not that, and you know it."

"Law." The way my name sat so sweetly on her berry-colored lips sent a thrill through me. "We would be a horrible fit," she finally stated after a lengthy pause.

"We would be a perfect fit," I argued.

"Law, I could never be the reason another woman's

happiest day turned into her own personal nightmare. I can't believe you would put the weight of your horrible timing on my shoulders."

I frowned, knowing that I hadn't thought this all the way through. It never occurred to me that Jackie might be seen as the proverbial bad guy if she agreed to be with me. Mostly, because I knew we'd never crossed a line before now.

"I also can't be the reason that you regret making the worst decision of your life. You and Bea are beautiful together." There was a wistfulness to her tone that made me think she had been a bit jealous of Bea.

"We're not, obviously, or I wouldn't be here right now."

Still, Jackie continued to break my heart as she finished speaking. "I could never be with someone who could do this to another woman. You are about to ruin Bea if you go through with this. She will never get over being left at the altar. Do you realize what you've left her to do? She has to go out there and discover that you're not there, in front of everyone that you both know and love."

I shook my head again. "No, I left a note with my best man. She will know before she's supposed to walk down the aisle."

Jackie gasped, as a horrified look slid over her face and her hands flew up to cover her gaping mouth. "No. Tell me you didn't leave her a note saying you were coming here to me!"

"I didn't put your name in it."

"But you left her, on your wedding day, with only a note that you had someone else deliver?" When I nodded slightly in confirmation she shook her head. "That's awful." The words were whispered. Then Jackie straightened her back and stood taller, while she glared me down.

"You need to go back. Either you marry that woman - if she'll still have you, or you take responsibility for your actions and you go tell all those people that you called off the wedding at the last, impossible minute. Bea shouldn't be stuck with cleaning up your mess after you dumped her on her wedding day." The disappointment in Jackie's eyes was what kicked me into gear.

"I really screwed this all up, didn't I?"

"You really did," she admitted. "If you had broken things off with her months ago, and then come to me today, I would have said yes. Now, I don't think I can stand to look at you again. Jesus, Law! What were you thinking?"

Shit! Fuck!

"Dammit, I…" The words were a jumble on my tongue. "I'm sorry," I told her as I backed up and headed for the door. I could see it in her eyes, though. I'd just fucked up my only shot at ever being with Jackie. Chances were, I'd also just fucked up any hope of getting Bea to walk down that aisle and marry me, but I had to go back and try because Jackie stood there and glared at me like I was a piece of steaming, odoriferous dog shit she'd just stepped in.

Todd had thrown a whiskey-filled flask at me that morning to help with the cold feet. Maybe, I should have drunk it before I fucked everything up. Instead, I downed the whole damn thing as I left my office building on the way back to the church. Even if I had to work to earn Bea's trust again, Jackie was right, I couldn't leave her to clean up the mess I made of my life.

It didn't take long to get back to the church. It was literally one block from the office where I'd gone to see Jackie. I'd been gone long enough that I thought people should have started to flood out of the church by then, though. That's why it was strange to hear The Wedding March play. Maybe Todd hadn't given Bea the letter. Hope lifted my spirit, and I ran up the stairs, into the lobby, and then through the door just as the usher was about to shut it.

"What's going on?" I whispered.

The usher - a kid that Bea had chosen for the position - smirked at me and then his smirk grew into a full-blown grin. "Snooze you lose, asshole!"

He didn't wait around for my response, instead he moved to take a seat in the back row of pews. It was then that my eyes drifted down the aisle to see Bea - my fiancee - walking arm-in-arm with her father toward the front of the church.

Her silky, cream-colored gown flowed behind her in tiny little ripples, like waves of silk on a gentle breeze. Her curly, dark hair was pulled back from her face with floral pins but left long and draping down the open back portion of her dress. I knew that she would have the face of an angel if I were to see her from the front, but that wasn't possible since she was walking away from me, down the aisle, toward someone else. How in the hell was that possible?

"What the fuck?" The words were obviously heard from the back pew because the kid turned around again and silently laughed at me while he shook his head.

Color me stunned as fuck when I moved a little to the left, so that I could see who was at the other end of the aisle. There, waiting to wed *my* fiancee with the dopiest grin known to man on his face, was Bea's lifelong best friend,

Kylan. He had also been known as one of the town's biggest players. According to Bea, he supposedly had a serious relationship at some point and had been burned by the woman. Ever since, he chose to play the field instead of settling down with anyone. Until now. Now, it looked like he had chosen the woman who was supposed to be *my* wife.

I don't know if I was too shocked to do anything, too curious if she would actually go through with it, or what; but I stood there and watched them go through with the entire ceremony. They even exchanged rings, and like fuck if I knew how in the hell they managed to have rings. I glanced over at my best friend who stood there in his position as best man. He looked just as blown away by the change of groom as I had. When they mentioned the rings he held his hand up slightly and caught my eye. He had them. Both rings. That meant the asshole, Ky, must have had a backup plan all along.

I wondered, briefly, if it had been his intention to hijack my wedding for himself, or if there was something else at play. The sad fucking reality was that I had absolutely no one to blame but myself. I set this in motion the minute I left that letter with Todd.

Chapter Three

KY

"Holy shit!"

Dammit, I shouldn't curse out loud in a church. I just left Bea in the dressing room with the fucking letter that prick gave her instead of showing up to marry the best woman on the damn planet. I gave myself five minutes to get shit right. What was I thinking?

"That's no way to speak in the house of the Lord, boy."

"Grandma?" I spun to find my petite grandmother as she stared me down with a glare that could freeze a grown man in his place. After a heartbeat, her lips finally eased and turned back up into a smile.

"The prick isn't showing up, is he?" She asked. I could chide her for using such language in the Lord's house, but I was short on time, so all I did was acknowledge that she'd read the situation correctly. Grandma reached up behind her neck with shaky hands and unclasped the necklace she always wore. It was a thick, white gold chain. Once she pulled it free of her dress, I saw that a ring dangled from the end.

"You take this, see if it fits." I grabbed the ring as she handed it to me and placed it on my left ring finger. There was no other possible finger it was supposed to go on, and damn. "Look at that, it's perfect," Grandma said as she clamped her hand down on top of mine. "Good, now go make today right for that girl, since you've been too stupid to get the job done before now."

Grandma left me as I stood gape-mouthed in shock while she retreated down the hall. "Foolish boy came so close to losing her…" She mumbled as she walked away. I took two steps before someone else halted my progress.

"Not so fast." I turned to see Bea's grandmother. I hadn't noticed her standing there in the shadows of the restroom door, but apparently she'd seen and heard everything that transpired between my grandma and me.

"Here." She held out her boney hand to me and dropped another, daintier ring into my palm. I noticed her ring finger was now bare and sported a tan line where her ring had once been. "It will fit her, I promise." She smiled at me even as she sniffled a little bit as moisture built in her rheumy eyes. "Looks like this was meant to be." She turned and followed after my grandma, having just given me her own wedding ring. The same ring that I knew for a fact she hadn't removed from her body since before her husband passed away.

I never had a doubt about what I was about to do, and now that both of our grandmothers had meddled and offered up two very important pieces that I'd need to make this happen, I knew what Bea's granna said was true. It was meant to be. I also knew what my grandma said was true, because if the prick hadn't gotten cold feet, I might have lost my chance at finally letting Bea know how I feel about her. How I've felt about her for far too long without doing anything about it.

The clock on the wall ticked another minute by and I got my butt in gear. There was somewhere I needed to be, and I only had two minutes to get there before everything would be ruined, so I ran. I ran down the aisle and right up to the minister who was waiting to marry my girl to another man. Like hell that would happen now.

"Listen, there has been a slight change in plans?"

"Oh?" He asked as he looked down his nose, past his glasses, and straight into my eyes with a knowing smile. What was it with all the retirement-age people in the church today? "Change the name of the groom for me, please."

"Son, you realize nothing will be legal if I do that today. There is paperwork that needs filling out."

I bobbed my head up and down quickly, knowing that we were about to run out of time. "I know. We can get it done afterward. It will still count then, right?"

"Of course, we'll make it work." He winked at me just as the organ off in the corner started playing the wedding march. "Better get in your new place, son." He tipped his head toward the opposite side of where I was supposed to stand as my best friend's bride's man. That was the title we'd given me, since I wasn't a fucking bridesmaid. Maybe the title was more appropriate than we thought because I was about to take a leap of fucking faith to see if my best friend would accept me to be her man in the most important way.

I whispered my name to the pastor, "Kylan Armstrong," and slid into place just as the door opened and took a deep breath to calm my rapidly beating heart. The moment Bea came into view, I knew that was a pointless effort. My heart stopped. Completely. It was a dead muscle in my chest and nothing more for a solid... Okay, well it probably only missed one beat, but that wasn't the point. My girl looked like an angel walking toward me in all her beautiful glory. The dress she chose fit her like a glove and made all her luscious curves stand out that much more inside the creamy satin.

Her dark, curly hair, that I loved to play with when Bea would tolerate it, was pulled away from her face but left long. I knew that the prick had requested she wear it up because his mother said only trash wore their hair down on their wedding day. I was happy to see that she had followed her heart. My Bea had never been a pushover though, so I expected no less from her than to do whatever the hell she wanted.

There was a time when I pictured myself marrying her, and in those moments of weakness, when I allowed myself to think about it, she always had her hair down. I never pictured the actual wedding. Maybe that made me weird, but I always pictured our lives further down the road, after the wedding, and in those imagined moments, a picture of us hung on the wall. She looked just as beautiful today, even more so, than in those fantasy images I had conjured.

I have always loved Bea. I've probably always been at least a little in love with her, too. I just couldn't ever admit it because my girl never saw me that way. I'd always only been her friend. I even tried to have a few relationships over the years in an effort to get her out of my heart and firmly into the friend zone where she kept me. Don't get me wrong, I knew that Bea loved me. Of course she did.

She had never been in love with me in a romantic way, though.

I allowed my fantasies to run away with me as she made her way toward me on her father's arm. At first, she glanced around, puzzled. I know she must have thought that I would somehow get Law to show up, but fuck that guy. He lost out on his chance, as far as I was concerned.

I imagined Bea knowingly walking toward me at the end of the aisle, instead of how she looked slightly confused, then resigned, before she tipped a small smile up at the corner of her lips. Her eyes were watery, and I wasn't sure if that was grief for the loss of the relationship she thought she was entering into today or if it was because her best friend was making sure her day wasn't completely ruined.

"What are you doing?" Bea whispered the minute her father slipped her hand into mine and gave her away to me.

"You're a good man," Sean said to me before he took a step back and then turned to head to his seat.

"What's it look like?" I asked Bea in a whisper. "I'm marrying you." Apparently, I didn't 'whisper' as quietly as I thought because the entire first two rows started to laugh. I lowered my voice and leaned in close to spell things out for just her. "Your family paid for all of this, and you look so stunning, Bea. I've loved you forever anyway, so this makes sense to me."

"But Law," she whispered back emphatically.

"Was a coward who left you with only a note on the day you were supposed to marry him. I'm right here. Take a chance on me, Bea. It was always supposed to be us together anyway." I took a chance telling her that and when I leaned back away from her again, with her hands still wrapped in my own, she glanced at the first row of seats where her family were situated. After seeing the smiles on their faces, and the tears in some eyes, she turned back to me and nodded.

The pastor went through our vows with us, and he didn't forget the name change, thank God. Was it okay to thank the big man in his house? Shit, I didn't know. Honestly, the vows were a blur with the exception of the moment when we exchanged rings.

"Do you have rings to exchange?" The pastor wisely asked since the whole groom swap had been a bit of shakeup. I nodded my head and handed the one that Bea was supposed to put on my finger to her.

"This was my grandfather's ring. He and my grandma were in love all the way up until he passed on without her, and then she wore this close to her heart every day after. I can only hope for the same amount of love and loyalty from you one day, and in return you won't have to hope for the same from me because it will be a given."

With shaky hands and tears streaming down her face, Bea pushed the ring onto my finger and held on tightly for a minute as she stared at it and took in the words I spoke. Then, it was my turn to place a ring on her finger.

"This was your granna's ring. I know you already know her love story with your granddad. We listened to her tell it together many times over the years. Your grandparents and mine have doubly blessed this union between us, Bea. I hope you're ready for forever, because that's the kind of love they put into their blessing." I slid the ring on her finger, and her granna had been right. It was a perfect fit. A tear dripped down onto my hand as I held Bea's steady. I glanced up into her watery eyes and her sweet smile took my breath from my lungs.

"By the power vested in me, I now pronounce you husband and wife," the pastor announced. He then turned slightly, so that he was facing me, as he gave the go ahead to do something I'd always wanted to do. "You may kiss *your* bride." I didn't miss the emphasis he put on that all important word. "Your."

Bea was mine.

I leaned in and wrapped my arms around her waist to tug her into me and then, our lips came together slowly, and I swear to God - it's okay because he knew - sparks flew between us. Electricity zinged through me, overwhelming my senses and the sensation forced me to deepen the kiss.

Cheers erupted through the crowd that had been gathered, but only from one side of the church. The other side, the one that held the groom's family, was silent as the grave until one voice rose above the cacophony of noise from the other side.

"No! Bea, no!"

My stomach dropped as I let go of Bea and we both turned to see Law as he stared at us from the back of the church looking absolutely gutted. The only thing that kept me from dissolving into the same barely able to stand, grief-stricken feeling that he was apparently immersed in, was that Bea never once let go of me. She stood with one hand clasped around my neck, the other around my waist, with her fingers splayed along my lower back. Instead of moving away, she pushed closer, begging me silently to hold her together through whatever was coming.

Oh, sweet Bea, you don't even have to ask. I'm never letting you go.

Chapter Four

BEA

Law was really there, at the opposite end of the aisle from where he should have been all along. I wondered for a moment if he'd seen the whole thing. Had he stood there and watched as I married my best friend? Was this all some game to him? Was I supposed to say 'no' to Kylan? No. That couldn't be true. I had Law's letter folded and tucked into the bodice of my wedding dress.

It was a reminder of what I needed to do once I got up here. Though, I thought Ky would have magically produced Law to stand there waiting for me. I had planned to tell him, in front of everyone, what he could do with his wedding. I had planned to read the letter to everyone to let them know what a callous asshole he had been. They all deserved to know what a coward he had been to leave me there to dispense the news on my own before my best friend stepped in. I had planned on leaving with Ky and throwing Law's letter back in his own face. I never thought I'd be married to Ky when we left though. That part had been a shocker.

Law ran down the aisle toward us as my father started

24

ushering some of the guests out of the church. "Bea! Please, I made a mistake!" Law yelled as he continued his journey.

"You sure did," I scolded him. Then when he stopped an arm's length away as I stood there, unwilling to remove myself from Kylan's arms, the scents clinging to Law hit me like a ton of bricks. The man smelled like whiskey and another woman's perfume.

"You smell like a whole affair right now, despite your letter's assurances that you never cheated on me. You know the absolute crap you wrote in that letter about how you were just leaving me on our wedding day because you were interested in another woman?"

I spat the words out and ignored the gasps that came from the audience. Both sides of the audience were apparently shocked to hear that Law had been the cause of the groom swap. I'm sure Law would hear it from his mother later. He had scandalized her, and after she already didn't approve of me to begin with.

"What?" Law finally asked, looking a little confused.

"You smell like whiskey and someone else's perfume," Ky informed him, taking the words right from my own mouth.

Law scoffed at him. "And you look like you just stole my girl."

"Can't steal what someone else gave away," Ky informed him.

"Can we not do this here, in front of God and everyone?" I asked. The pastor was the one who directed us to a small room off to the back of the church that was supposed to have been used by Law for any last-minute things he needed prior to the ceremony.

As soon as the door shut behind us, Law asked, "Bea, how could you?"

"How could I? Are you serious right now? You left me a note! A freaking NOTE, Law! You didn't even have the courage to say it to my face - preferably before our wedding day. My parents paid for everything here and you couldn't even respect them enough to tell me you were having doubts whenever you first started having them."

"I'm sorry, Bea. I was just confused."

"Clearly," I admonished.

"But I'm here now. It was a momentary lapse before I realized how wrong I was."

"Yeah?" I asked, growing angrier by the second. "Where were you then?" The look of guilt on his face revealed the truth that he was trying to dance around. "Let me guess, whoever she is, you went to see her, and she rejected you." I laughed because the picture was painted clearer as I spoke and watched as the guilt wrote the truth he was afraid to tell all over his face. "Suddenly, you came to your senses and made your way back here to me. I guess, at the very least, you got a parting hug from her since you smell like another woman. Then, you went and drowned your sorrows in whiskey before you decided to settle on the one you were supposed to marry today. Does that sound about right?"

"Bea, it's not like that," he cried and there were actual tears, too. Part of me wanted to hold and comfort him because it seemed like what his fiancee should do. Then, I remembered why I'd just married my best friend instead of him. I moved away from Law and back into Ky's arms. My best friend - husband - didn't even hesitate to pull me against the warmth of his body and offer whatever comfort and strength I needed. That was how it was supposed to be, right?

"I only had a case of nerves, Bea. You literally married someone else. I thought you were both *'just friends'* all this time. That's been your party line all along whenever I questioned how close the two of you were. Maybe I should ask how long you've been together behind my back?"

"A few minutes ago, on the altar, was the first time my lips have ever touched Kylan's. We have always, only, ever been friends - until today when you wrote me a cowardly note and Ky stepped in to save *my* day."

It was the truth. My best friend was a handsome man, no doubt. There had been moments throughout our friendship where I thought there could have been more between us, but I always shied away, afraid of losing the amazing friendship we had if we screwed it up with a relationship.

"So, just like that, you go from me to marrying my replacement? It was really that easy?"

"You think any part of this day has been easy?" He stood and stared at me cluelessly as I whisper-hissed those words. "And what would have happened if that woman had said 'yes' to you? Would you have even cared that I married my best friend today when my fiancé didn't show up to do it?"

"Bea, that's not fair." He argued. It only caused me to laugh at him again.

"None of this seems to be fair, but it all stems from *your* actions. Stop blaming me, and you can stop blaming Ky, too. *You* set all of this in motion with that stupid letter that you didn't even have the guts to give me yourself."

"And he just happened to have rings on him to trade

with you today?" Law scoffed as he slid narrowed, judging eyes on Kylan.

"Law, our grandmothers gave me their rings when they noticed you weren't going to be here to marry Bea today."

Law's jaw dropped. It was one thing to think that Kylan and I had just married, but it was another for him to know that my family was behind making it happen. Law thought my family adored him. They did - to a point. They adored the fact that he seemed to love and respect me. That adoration stopped the minute he decided not to show up for our wedding. That was before they knew it was because of another woman. I couldn't imagine what they were all thinking now that they'd heard me call him out on what he'd done.

"Bea," Law pleaded again.

I shook my head. "Even if I hadn't married Ky just now, we would have been over the minute I read your note. You were right. If you were interested enough in someone else to call off our wedding, on the day of the event no less, then we weren't meant to be together anyway."

"I just got nervous!" Law yelled at me.

"You will not yell or scream at her," Ky growled as he stepped up and tucked me further behind his body. "Bea has been through enough, and she's right. You knew when you wrote those words how Bea would take them. You had to have known that once you put those words in her hands it would be completely over. If you didn't factor that into what you did here today, then you have never really known the woman you supposedly wanted to marry."

I don't know if it was adrenaline starting to wane, heartbreak setting in, or just the numbness finally leaving me and allowing my feelings to return, but my legs started to shake just as my father and brother entered the room.

"Come on, Law" My dad called out to him as he and Flynn helped to pluck Law up from where he'd just fallen to his knees. "Take a few days, think things through, and then try talking again if you guys need to say anything else to one another." We watched as my family dragged Law from the room, and for the first time since Ky told me to meet him at the altar, we were alone.

"Why?" I asked him.

Ky was still faced away from me, as he watched Law being escorted out. His shoulders moved up and down once before he swiveled around to look me in the eyes. "I don't want you to hate me if I tell you the truth."

"I could never hate you."

"The thought of you marrying him made me sick, Bea. I went along with it because you seemed happy, and that's all I ever wanted for you, but…"

"What does that mean?"

"I don't know when I first fell in love with you," he admitted, and that admission took my breath away. Still, he continued. "I could pinpoint a thousand moments that could have been it, but the truth is they all just added up to me falling deeper for you through the years."

"You never said anything," I accused.

"I never really had the chance." He chuckled before the rest of his explanation came tumbling out. "I planned to take you to dinner and tell you, but then you never showed up. It was the day your car broke down and you met Law."

"Oh, Ky!" I gasped as understanding dawned. I remembered gushing about my 'knight in shining armor' the next day and how he had asked me out and of course, I'd agreed after the handsome do-gooder and his friend Todd had saved me from the side of the road. I dug into my memories of that moment and the reality of the situation hit me hard. My dearest friend had seemed sad about something, instead of excited for me. "When I asked you why you were upset, you said you'd just been dumped by a girl who you liked a lot."

"Yeah, Bea, because that's what it felt like - knowing I had just lost my shot with you again."

"Why didn't you just tell me?"

"It was clear, by how excited you were over Law, that you never felt the same way about me."

I sighed as I moved into his arms, and wrapped my own around his waist as I rested my head against his chest. "You should have told me. I was excited about Law because he was new, interested, and someone to take my mind off you and the women who were in and out of your life." I looked up to my friend, my new husband for all intents and purposes. "If I had known that date with Law would have never happened."

It was as close to the truth as I could get, because Ky was so far off the mark by saying I wasn't interested, that it was insane. I had always thought the reverse was true, that he had never been interested in me beyond friendship.

"Are you serious?" He asked.

"Yes. It's not that I've never felt attracted to you, Ky. I've just always valued our friendship. Neither of us ever had a lasting relationship before, and I didn't want to lose you if we didn't work out romantically."

"I guess we kind of have to see it through now, huh?"

He teased, but I wasn't so sure that was true either. We'd said our vows, exchanged rings, and kissed, but marriage had legalities mixed up in it, too. My marriage license had Law's name on the paperwork, not Ky's.

"Are you sure you want this, Ky?"

"Are you?" Ky took hold of my hands and rubbed his finger over my ring. "He might have gotten cold feet and wrote a stupid letter, but he came back for you."

I rolled my eyes. "He only came back after he supposedly wrote twenty-two variations of that letter and had it delivered by someone else. Let's not forget that he also ran off to see another woman, started drinking after she rejected him, and only then did he show up again. You were right. The moment I received that letter, there was no going back to him. I won't be his fallback plan because what he really wanted didn't pan out."

"What does that make me then?" He asked.

"My best friend – always. My husband – maybe."

"Maybe?" Ky questioned as a deep frown marred his handsome face.

"You do realize that what we did out there isn't legal, right?" He didn't seem surprised by that question, which meant he'd already thought about it to some extent. "There's paperwork involved, a license to obtain, and…"

"Do you want it to be legal?" Ky asked as he pushed one of my curls that had fallen down around my face back behind my ear.

"Do you?"

"Of course, I do, Bea. This was a lot for you today though, so maybe you should think about it first." I smiled at him then.

"Well, it's Friday, any paperwork would have to wait until Monday anyway."

"What now?"

"There's the reception," I answered hollowly, not sure I wanted to face everyone after marrying a different man than they originally came to see.

"I won't leave your side, if you want to go."

"I appreciate that, but what are we supposed to tell people?"

"That you realized I was the real man of your dreams all along?" I don't know why, but his playful suggestion started a chain reaction. First, the tears fell hot and wet down my face, and then the sobbing began. "Did I do the wrong thing here, Bea?" Ky's voice was soft and unsure as he asked. I hated it because it was so unlike him.

"No, Ky. I just need a minute to fall apart. No matter what, Law and I were together for two and a half years. It's just that..." I couldn't put into words what I was feeling. Maybe, the shock was finally wearing off and it was just dawning on me what everything meant. Law was no longer mine, and I was certainly no longer his. And then there was Ky and what it might mean if our impromptu nuptials didn't work out. I couldn't lose him, too.

Chapter Five

BEA

"I UNDERSTAND, there's no pressure here, Bea."

Ky's words melted into my heart because he never said something he didn't mean. Even though I just told him that I needed a minute to come to terms with everything and wrap my head around all the changes that the day had brought, I still snuggled into his arms. He didn't protest or throw a fit about how unfair things were that I was in his arms while crying over another man. He was simply there for me in whatever capacity I needed him to be.

Pastor Bob Gordon, poked his head into the room and I almost panicked at the thought that he would kick us out. He held his hand out as if seeing the worry written on my face.

"You can stay as long as you like. I'll be around until nine tonight and nothing else is going on that you would interfere with. The girls are cleaning everything up. I just came in to let you know that my secretary is working on the new certificates. If you want to obtain a license on Monday, we can sign all the paperwork after you bring it in and then we can file it with the courts to make everything legal." He cleared his throat a moment before tacking on, "Assuming that's what you both want to do."

I nodded my head and Bob slipped back out the door. "What do you think?" I asked Kylan.

"I think I just told you, 'No pressure', so I'm going to stick by that." His honesty made me chuckle. "Let's just wait until the weekend is over, and if you feel like making a decision then, we'll talk it over and do what's right for both of us."

"That is why you have remained my best friend for so long."

"Because I'm agreeable?"

"No, because you genuinely care about other people before you worry about yourself."

"Well, as you've seen, that hasn't always been the best course of action." I knew he meant what he'd told me earlier – about not telling me his true feelings when Law came into the picture. He'd done it to see to my happiness, but at his own expense. As it turned out, it might have been at both of our expense.

The door opened again, causing me to startle. It was like I had PTSD and expected Law to come bursting through the doors to demand that I marry him while he dates other people. I shook the awful thought off as my mother poked her head around the corner.

"Bea," she said then turned her eyes up over my shoulder to where Ky still sat with me wrapped in his arms. "Ky," she added. "Do you think you could give me a moment alone with my daughter?"

Ky squeezed his arms around my waist a bit first before he whispered in my ear. "Is that okay with you?"

"Yeah, it's fine," I confirmed before patting his hand and then letting go so he could remove his hold on me. Ky stood and walked toward my mother without looking back.

"I'll be right outside if she needs me," he told her as he walked out of the room. Ky didn't get to see the smile his words put on my mom's lips, but I did. When she saw that I noticed, she immediately schooled her features and walked over to where I'd been sitting on a step that raised the floor level a few inches higher, almost as if they'd been trying to make a stage in the room. It was actually the first time I realized that I'd been seated on a multi-level floor. Weird how those details that seem so huge escape your notice when your world had just been turned upside down,.

"That boy would guard you from hell itself," my mom mentioned as she took a seat beside me. I nodded because it was probably true so there was no point in arguing. "Is this what you want?" My mother finally asked. As if the question was that simple to answer.

"I was in love with Law," I admitted.

"Well, I figured as much, since you agreed to marry him." There was no judgment in my mother's voice, but there was also no joy. My family had liked Law well enough, but they'd never been excited that I was with him. For some reason, I thought maybe that just wasn't a thing.

Whenever I'd tell them Law was coming home with me to dinner, they'd say things like, *"Okay, see you both there."* I guess I always expected more. Maybe because whenever I'd tell them Ky was coming, their responses were always more along the lines of, *"Fabulous, I haven't seen Ky in weeks!"*

"Oh, great, I had something I've been meaning to talk to him about."

"Fantastic, I've missed his charming, dimpled smile."

I always figured they'd grow to love Law the same way, eventually.

I pulled the note from my bodice and handed it to my mother. "Todd brought that to me before the ceremony."

Mom gasped as she read it and then pulled me in for a tight hug. "That bastard had these doubts, these thoughts for another woman, and he couldn't be bothered to say something before today? That bastard!"

I wanted to laugh at her use of "bastard" twice in a row because my mom was not one to use vulgar language. Mom tossed the paper, but I quickly snatched it up knowing that I would need the reminder of his actions over the next few days. Hanging onto my anger was imperative.

"If he was here, right now, I would put my foot so far up that son of a bitch's ass that he would taste the leather on my shoes."

I giggled. "Mom, we're still in church."

"I'm sure the good Lord can forgive my sins knowing what that man put you through today. I'm just so angry on your behalf."

We sat in comfortable silence for a few moments, as my mom waited me out. "I don't know what the right thing is here."

"Do you love him?"

"Who?"

She tilted her head to the side as if to ask, 'really?'. "Kylan."

"I've always loved him," I admitted, but she knew there

was a difference between loving someone and being in love with them.

"Do you think he'd ever pull a stunt like Law did and leave you in the lurch?"

I gasped at the suggestion. "Absolutely not."

She made a sound in the back of her throat, that I supposed was her agreeance. "Then it sounds to me like he's the one you should hitch your horse to."

"Mom, if things don't work out..."

"I'm going to stop you right there, daughter of mine. That man has already proved what he's willing to do for you. Even if you're not in love with him right this minute, that doesn't mean you won't be later on and again sometime down the road. Do you think I've been 'in love' with your father throughout our whole marriage?"

I was stunned to hear her ask that question. "What does that mean?"

"Sweetie, love doesn't work that way. There have been times when I have tolerated being with your father, others where I loathed the man, and many where I was giddy in love with him. Through it all, I loved him, but that feeling you're sinking your teeth into – the one stopping you from really examining your relationships – is fleeting.

"If you're lucky, you will continually fall in and out of love with the man you marry for the rest of your lives. The kicker, the way to weigh whether he's worth it, is by how much you try to make one another happy through it all. Being 'in love' is a hormone rush. Having love for someone means respect, patience, forgiveness, and work. It means having the strong foundation to make falling in love over and over again possible." Her left brow pushed up in that familiar way it always did when she asked one of her children if we understood her.

"I get it."

"Good. Now," she said while her eyes darted around the room, "I have it on good authority that there's a bathroom in here." She stood and dusted her butt off. "Ah, there it is. I'll be right back." My mom struggled to make haste to the bathroom which caused me to laugh, because the woman was notorious for her weak bladder. She'd probably been holding it since before the ceremony, afraid she'd miss something.

My bouquet, which had been long forgotten, sat there discarded on the steps beside me. Apparently, my mother managed to salvage it from wherever it had been abandoned. I couldn't even remember if I'd been carrying it down the aisle with me, but I didn't think so. It had one solitary pink rose in the center that was surrounded by white tulips and bound together with a pink ribbon. Tulips were my favorite flowers and the bouquet had been one more thing that Law's mother demanded I not use for my wedding.

The flower was more of a weed – in her words – and should never be seen at a wedding that her son took place in. Considering her snobby butt didn't kick over one dime for our wedding costs, I told her that she didn't get a say in what I chose for my wedding. Law had been angry with me, saying there was no need to get confrontational, and that I could have just gone with all roses instead.

That memory made me think hard about whether my ex-fiancé ever really knew me at all. He had been wearing a white rose bud in his lapel earlier when I'd seen him. Kylan had been wearing a tulip.

I stood and moved quickly to the door, needing to see my best friend, because I couldn't decide if I'd been imagining it or if it was true. If true, he would have caught hell for the choice while I was in the back room getting ready. Law's mother – and my fiancé – had been under the wrong impression that I changed my mind and went with all roses.

The door to the room was cracked and I heard voices on the other side which halted my steps. I felt I earned the right to eavesdrop on people after what happened to me on my wedding day. Apparently, I needed to be privy to more conversations people weren't aware that I could overhear, since I had no clue who in the hell Law had been so enamored with that he left me alone on our wedding day.

"I've been in love with Bea for a long time," Ky said. "I'm sorry I didn't do things the right way, Sean." He spoke to my father with an air of regret in his words. What did he mean by 'doing things the right way'?

"Son, when it comes to loving a woman, the only 'right way' is to do everything in your power to make sure she is happy. It bothered her that Law didn't want her to have her grandmother's ring. It was offered. Did you know?" I couldn't see Ky, but he must have shaken his head because my dad continued telling him about it. "When Law came to ask for her hand in marriage – at Bea's request – the ring was offered to him. He refused it and said that 'his wife wouldn't be wearing hand-me-down jewelry'."

"What an ass," Ky muttered. My father and another man's laughter rang out on the other side of the door.

"Well, as true as that is, she has the ring she truly wanted now, and that's thanks to you. It's fitting that her best friend gave it to her. My daughter might be hurt and confused for a while, but I have to believe that everything fell into place exactly the way it was meant to."

A quiet fell over the people on the other side of the door for a moment until my father spoke again. "What are you guys going to do about Bea's things?"

"Her things?" Ky asked.

"Flynn and Beckett just spent several days last week moving all of her things to Law's condo, so it would be set up once they got back from their honeymoon," Dad informed him.

"Shoot!" I huffed under my breath. That was one more thing I would have to straighten out. It also meant there was no way I could avoid seeing Law again. I wasn't in a financial position to just walk away from everything I'd worked so hard for, like my entire wardrobe for starters.

"I don't know," Ky answered honestly. "I think that will be up to Bea, but I'm not sure she needs one more burden on her shoulders today. Maybe, it can wait until tomorrow?" It sounded like more of a question than a suggestion. "If not, I guess we can all go over and pick it up for her. It's just a matter of where she wants it all taken."

"Don't beat yourself up over something you can't control," Ky's father suggested. I guess he had been the one laughing with them a minute ago. "While I'm happy you finally got your girl, I'm not so sure the rest will be as easy as all that. Just play it by ear and we'll all be on stand-by, in case you need us."

"You got that right," my father agreed. "We're here for you, Ky, but you know – where I'm concerned, my daughter comes first. So, whatever she wants, I'm going to respect her wishes." I'm not sure what happened after that, if Ky looked confused, or what, but my father quickly added to his sentiment. "I'm rooting for you, Son. I never thought Law was good enough for her. Besides, my wife has been planning for the two of you to be together eventually. I guess that woman knew what she was talking about. I shouldn't have doubted her."

A giggle behind me clued me in that I wasn't the only eavesdropper in the church. My mom was back from the bathroom and had at least overheard the last part.

"It's true. I always knew he was the one for you."

Chapter Six

BEA

I was shocked to hear that my father thought Law wasn't good enough for me, but more so to realize my mother thought I should end up with Ky all this time. She had never said a word to me. It amazed me that my parents put up the money for this whole ceremony when both of them apparently thought it was a mistake.

"Mom," I whispered as I turned fully to face her. "I'm so sorry."

"For what, sweetie?"

"All the money you guys spent. The wedding. The reception that we're not even attending right now. Oh, God. I feel awful."

"Stop that right now," she insisted. "My darling daughter, if we spent all this money today just so you could finally realize you were with the wrong man all along, then it was worth every darn penny."

My mom offered up one of her quick hugs, placed a kiss on my cheek, and then said her farewells to me. "Speaking of the reception, I need to head over there and make sure everything is going smoothly for the guests who showed up."

"What do you mean by 'for the guests who showed up'? |

Mom chuckled. "Well, I doubt Law's family felt inclined to celebrate your eventual nuptials to a man who wasn't their kin." Mom turned and walked out the door then, though I could have sworn I heard her mumble, "Serves them right for being assholes."

Despite my mother's departure, I wasn't left alone. My little sister, Mina, had quietly slipped into the room just prior to our mom taking off. I imagined Mom just wanted to give us some space so we could have sisterly bonding time over my epic day.

Mina made it pretty clear right away that she had not overheard anyone else's conversations. "I love Ky, you know that." It was the first thing she said to me before she decided to let me know that she thought I was the bad guy in this situation. "How could you do that to Law? Was it just because he was a little late to the wedding? You decided, if he couldn't be there on time, then to hell with him, you'll marry someone else?"

I was taken aback by my sister's tirade, especially since she didn't have a clue what she was talking about. It did make me wonder what everyone who attended the ceremony thought, though. I supposed not everyone heard what I had to say to Law when he walked up to us at the altar after I exchanged vows with Kylan instead. Maybe they all thought Ky and I were the worst sort of humans.

"You don't understand, Mina."

"I understand that you betrayed the man you pledged to

marry and made him look like a complete fool in front of absolutely everyone."

I wanted to throttle my sister. She was always so black and white in the way she thought things through. I loved her dearly, but once she set her mind to something, there was rarely any changing it. Still, there was no way I would take the brunt of her wrath for something that should be focused on my ex-fiancé.

"No! You don't understand." I raised my voice at my sister before I ripped the letter Law had written me back out of my bodice again. I really wished the dress had pockets because I hated keeping the damn thing so close to my heart, but there was nowhere else to tuck it away. I had still been holding my bridal bouquet and a few of the rose petals dislodged and fell away in my haste. I handed the folded page to Mina and watched as she read the reminder I had of Law's fickle love. It was a good reminder too, one that made me steadfast in the decision I'd make with Ky today.

"He sent this to you? Today?" When I nodded, full understanding dawned in my sister's eyes. "That's why he was late? He went to this other woman?"

My sister dropped to her butt, and sat on the floor – not even the raised section that made more sense as a seat. Her beautiful dress would most likely be ruined by the end of the day.

"Yet another reason to never trust love – it lies," she mumbled, obviously fighting her own internal battles that I sadly knew nothing about.

"Mina, no. It doesn't lie. Not when it's right and real. Look at Mom and Dad or Grandma Grace and Poppy Thomas.

They all have incredible love stories." It was almost ironic that the jilted bride was the one standing there trying to convince her sister that love was real, and yet there I was doing just that.

"Maybe, but I don't think it exists anymore. I swear to you, Bea, if I ever marry, it won't ever be for love."

"Don't say that." I insisted.

"Why not? Look at you! Married out of heartbreak, not love."

"That's not true either. I love Kylan." It was only as I said it to my sister that I was able to acknowledge the truth. I did love Ky. I'd been in a position to love two men at once, but the stronger of those loves had always been the one I had for my best friend. When Mina looked as though she didn't believe me, I decided to tell her a secret.

"Law once asked me to give up Ky because he thought Ky was in love with me," I admitted.

"He did? But you didn't agree to that, obviously."

I shook my head. "No, I could never. I told Law that he didn't want to force me to choose between them because it would never turn out in his favor."

"What if you gave up your true love for your best friend?"

"Do you think my true love would leave me a note like that," I pointed to the paper still held in her hand, "on our wedding day?" She didn't answer, just handed the damned thing back to me. "Besides, I thought you didn't believe in true love," I teased.

"I thought you loved Law," she hit back.

"I did, Mina. I love Ky more though. I could never imagine my life without him."

"Then maybe you did the right thing." Mina sat thoughtfully as she spoke. "Have you and Ky ever…"

I shook my head in response, knowing where she was going with the question before she even finished.

"Won't that be weird then?"

"What?"

"Sex with the boy who has been your best friend since before you knew you liked boys in that way. It's your wedding day, Bea. You're supposed to have sex with him to seal the deal."

It was my turn to plop my butt on the floor beside my sister. Why hadn't I thought of that? The bag I had packed for my honeymoon with Law was filled with all sorts of lingerie to tempt him with. A warm blush stole across my cheeks as I thought of wearing any of it for Ky to see.

"What if you're no good together in bed?" Mina asked, and I swear if she wasn't my sister, I would beat the crap out of her for making me think of these things, and for making me doubt myself and Ky. She must have noticed my panicked expression and her reaction to that was to laugh. "Good to know you really thought all this through, Bea."

"I haven't fantasized like that about Ky in years," I told her honestly, ignoring the jab about thinking things through, because it was already obvious that I'd walked down that aisle on a spur of the moment decision and nothing more than faith in my best friend to make everything right.

"You used to?"

"Of course, have you seen him?" We both giggled over my admission. "I used to imagine us together all the time in high school. I wanted him to be my first," I told her.

"Then why wasn't he?"

"I tried to tell him once, but just as I was going to admit my feelings to him, I walked in on him having sex with Olivia Dennings instead."

"Oh Bea!" My sister cooed as she wrapped an arm around my shoulders. "Did he at least feel bad about it?"

I shook my head once more and stared at my hands that were folded up in my lap. The glint of light on my ring felt like a lie as I spoke about the past. "He never knew I was there."

"Wait, was that your junior year?"

"How did you know?"

My sister squeezed my shoulders again. "Because now I understand why you turned him down for prom and then pretended to be sick so you wouldn't have to watch as he danced with Olivia."

My sister was right. That's exactly what happened. When Ky asked me, two days after I'd seen him naked and inside of Olivia, I informed him that I already had a date to prom. It was a lie, of course, but one he didn't even question. Instead, he got angry with me and demanded to know who was taking me. I refused to tell him. Then he turned around and asked Olivia to go with him to prom, and he did it right in front of me. That was the day I truly knew we could never be more than friends because it would ruin everything. I knew it to be true because a piece of my heart took a beating that year, and for a while, I wasn't sure our friendship would survive it. Seeing him after everything that happened already hurt beyond measure.

"He had so many girlfriends and hookups after that," my sister mumbled, as if she had read where my thoughts were headed.

"And each one broke my heart further until we went to college, and I met Jacob Stanley." We dated for three years, until he graduated the year before me and moved back home to California. I didn't want to move so far away from my family, and certainly didn't want to have to transfer schools in my final year, so we broke up and went our separate ways.

"So, Jacob was your first then?"

"Yes, and then I didn't date anyone else until Law came around."

"Wait! So, you've only been with two men?"

"Yes," I admitted. "I never wanted to be like the girls Ky used and discarded so frequently. I couldn't. Sex means something to me."

"Wow!" I didn't know why my sister was so surprised. I was no prude but knew enough that sex and emotion were inseparable for me.

A man's laughter caught our attention, and we turned to see Law standing there laughing as Kylan's face drained of color. Law slapped Ky on the back. "Looks like I have your dirty dick to thank for the two and a half years I've had with Bea. Thanks, man. Maybe now that she remembers why she was never with you, she'll realize exactly what I did, after her family threw me out earlier. You two aren't legally married. You can't be because you never filed the paperwork."

Ky didn't even object or say anything else to anyone. He simply turned and left.

I watched as Law's smug face turned to watch him go before moving back in my direction. "I forgive you for walking down the aisle to him and for pretending to marry him to prove your point to me. I get it. I fucked up. Come on, Bea. We can move on from this now."

"For how long exactly?" I asked as my voice wobbled on the emotion building under the surface.

"We were going to pledge ourselves to one another until death do us part, remember?"

"Yes, we were going to do that, but then you left me a note about another woman who caught your eye. So, how long until the next one? How long until one of them agrees to be with you and I receive another cowardly note?"

"Bea! Please, it was just cold feet."

"Did you, or did you not, leave me a note on the day of our wedding and run off to see another woman?"

"Bea!" He pleaded.

"Did you go see another woman on our wedding day?" I yelled the question at him that time. He nodded his head in lieu of a verbal answer. "Right," I agreed. "We are done, Law. I can never trust you again after that. I understand having doubts and cold feet, but you never talked to me about it. Sure, you may not have cheated on me, but you left me on our wedding day with a note and went to see if this other woman returned your interest. That's just as bad. I had no idea. I was blindsided on my wedding day. Those doubts didn't just happen today. We could have worked through it, postponed or canceled the wedding if need be, if only you'd said something sooner. Instead, you humiliated me, you broke my trust in you, and that isn't something I can just move past." I took the time to stand then, so I would be on my feet when I finished. "My family will be by soon to collect my things from your condo."

"I know that I screwed up, Bea, but are we really

throwing two and a half years together away because I got spooked?"

"No, you threw it all away when another woman turned your head, you refused to ignore it, and then left me a note on our wedding day," I reiterated to him. "Why are you not getting this?" I huffed in frustration. "I can't trust you anymore. There is no relationship without trust."

"Law, I think it would be best for everyone involved if you all had some breathing room and time to think things through. This all just happened today. It's still fresh and still hurts," my sister counseled him, showing wisdom beyond her experience.

Law stood there, eyes moving back and forth between my sister and me. "Fine," he grumbled. "Don't send anyone for your things yet. Promise me that you'll think about it for a while first." I nodded in agreement. "And Bea, I can forgive your wedding tantrum with Ky because of what I did to initiate it, but if you make it official, that really will be the end of us." After that pompous-ass proclamation he left.

"The nerve of him," my sister growled. "He went off to be with someone else today and only came back because she obviously turned him down. Then he tells you not to move on or else you're finished?" She made an odd noise before adding, "I wish I was British."

"What?" I asked, wondering if my sister had just lost all her senses. "Why?"

"Then I could call him a bloody wanker without sounding like a poser. It needs to be authentic, Bea!" For the first time that day, I laughed so hard I thought I might pee in my panties. My sister's ridiculousness was just what I needed to hear at that moment. She must have known it because she grinned widely as she got to her feet and threw her arms around me.

"I love you. You're the best big sister in the world, and I think you'll be much happier now that you are no longer with him." It was a change from the way she defended him earlier, but I'd take it. At least my sister was capable of admitting when she'd been wrong.

"Because he's a bloody wanker?"

She winked at me and grinned. "Now, who's the poser?"

Chapter Seven

KY

I HAD NEVER FELT like such a piece of shit in all my life. Leaving, to get some fresh air and process, was the only option I had after I heard what Bea said about our past. She was right. I never knew that she was there. Worse, all those girls I ran through back then were some fucked up way for me to punish my best friend, and myself, for turning me down for prom.

My eyes stayed glued to the church doors, even as my thoughts wandered back to that prom. The last person I wanted to be there with was Olivia fucking Dennings. It was supposed to be Bea on my arm. All night, my eyes stayed glued on the gym doors. I'd been waiting for Bea to come through them, so that I could see who in the hell beat me to asking her to prom. I wanted to beat the shit out of whoever it was. As the night wore on, and Olivia got bored with me keeping watch for Bea, it became clearer that she wasn't coming. Every boy I knew that she interacted with was there. Her friends were, too. So, she wasn't coming with them as a group.

I always wondered what happened, and if she was stood up by whoever was supposed to be her date. I never had the guts to ask her, though I overheard her tell one of the other girls that she hadn't been feeling well and canceled. My stomach coiled tightly as I thought about the real reason she hadn't gone to her prom. Me. I'd fucked up.

The door to the church opened and caught my eye. Law headed my way, since he was parked just a few cars down from me. The smug grin from earlier was no longer plastered on his douche-level frat-bro face. While he got closer, I kept watching him, and wondered what the hell Bea had ever seen in the asshole. No one liked him. It was like she had blinders on that kept her from seeing his real personality. Then again, she knew my personality, but not the reasons I'd always whored myself around town.

Looking back, I realized that was another negative in my column. Law was a self-proclaimed monogamist before he met Bea. Supposedly, he had only had three girlfriends in his life and two of them had left him while the third was an amicable breakup. I knew all this because my best friend overshared all the things that killed me to hear over the last three years. Bea was his fourth. I couldn't even give her a number because I'd never kept count. It wasn't rockstar level, by any means, but I hadn't been a saint.

As soon as Law was close enough, I stepped back out of my car. The asshole didn't miss the movement and turned to size me up.

"You want to brawl in the parking lot now?" He asked. I shook my head. "Warn me to stay away from Bea?" Again, I shook my head. "What then?"

"If you think me coming out here for some air, so I

didn't bash your fucking skull in was me giving up, you're wrong." Law stared at me without saying anything in response. "I don't have to tell you to back off, stay away, or not to speak to her again. Do you know why?"

"Why is that, Kylan?" His voice dripped with disdain as his eyes narrowed on me in a way that spoke of impending violence if he didn't like my answer.

"The minute that letter touched Bea's hands, and she read those words that you wrote, she was done with you. Bea isn't the type of woman who takes that shit lightly. You thought it bothered me in there, hearing what she had to say about a part of our history I was clueless about. It should have taught you one thing – Bea puts herself first when her heart is on the line. She's not like the women out there who roll over and just take shit from someone and wait for more to roll around."

"She forgave you."

I shook my head for a third time. "No. Our friendship suffered, and I never even knew why until now. You think Bea and I are close, but we were far closer before I fucked it all up back then. Only, now it makes sense. She let go of a piece of me that she didn't think she could have back then, and she never looked back. We've known one another since we were knee high. What do you think that means for you, as the man who cowardly left her with a note while you went to meet up with another woman on your wedding day?"

"Fuck you, man! The thing you don't understand is Bea only had a childhood crush on a friend back then with you. She is in love with me, ready to marry me."

"Was."

"What?"

"She *was* in love with you. She *was* ready to marry you. Past tense, asshole. You sealed your fate by the way you handled your business and I'm just petty enough to tell you that you're a fucking idiot. You were willing to throw Bea away for a crush on that girl from your work."

Law paled and took a step back as if I'd physically struck him. I laughed in response. "Wondering how I know?" He gave the slightest tilt of his head that I took for an affirmative answer. "Every time we were out as a group, your eyes tracked Jackie. When she sat side-by-side with your fiancé, it wasn't Bea you were staring at. It was her."

"Bullshit. If you really saw that, then you would have told your bestie all about it, so she would leave me."

"Nah. Bea's not dumb. I trusted her to make her own decisions about you. She knew. She's been having her own doubts, asshole. The thing about my bestie is that she understood they were just doubts while you were willing to throw her away for a maybe situation. What happened? Did your maybe turn you down?"

"That's not your business."

"She likes Bea. She might have liked you too, but I'm guessing she was appalled that you would come to her on the day of your wedding instead of handling shit before it got that far."

Law retreated another step, confirming what I'd guessed. There was only one reason he came back to the church for Bea, and that was because he had been shot down. "You're a real piece of work, you know that? Did you honestly think Bea would wait around to be your backup plan after that letter?"

"Like you're any different. You left her swinging in the

wind too because you couldn't give up easy pussy for the girl you supposedly loved."

"I was a teenager back then, and you got that situation all wrong anyway. The real difference between you and me is that my number one concern is for Bea while you worry about yourself."

I turned away from Law and got back in my car. He stood there staring at the church, and while I could see the regret and loss painted all over his face, there wasn't a single cell in my body that felt bad for the dick. He deserved everything he had to face.

I took off for Bea's family's house because I knew that was where she would end up. The time apart would give us both some time to think things through and figure our own shit out, especially after the revelation I overheard. Law wasn't the only man with regrets where my best friend was concerned.

Chapter Eight

BEA

I HAD no apartment to go home to.

Despite the multiple conversations about my things being stored in Law's apartment, that was the one thing that hadn't sunk in. I didn't even have an empty apartment to go home to. The keys had been turned in yesterday and I stayed in a hotel suite just down the block last night. Normally, in a situation like this, I would call on my best friend. Ky had a couch I'd slept on plenty of times. The truth was, I couldn't call on him for this.

I wasn't even sure why he'd left. Yes, I had discussed how him being with someone else in high school had messed us up for a bit, and how I only ever slept with two people because I didn't want to be like those other women who could hop from man to man the way they did. More power to them, it just wasn't my thing. Maybe some considered it a flaw that I couldn't separate my feelings from sex, but if that's what it was, then I was fine being flawed.

I knew the things Law said to Ky had hit hard, especially after finding out that Law was the reason Kylan never came clean with me about his feelings in the first place. Still, Law said those things, not me. I kind of felt abandoned all over again. I didn't blame my friend though, it had been a crazy, emotional roller coaster of a day for everyone.

It still left me with one real option. I had to go home, to my parents' house, and that was the last place I wanted to be while nursing a heartbreak. Multiple heartbreaks? I didn't know. I just knew that my heart hurt, my head wasn't too far behind, and my legs didn't want to hold my body up any longer. The floor of the damn church started to look a little too inviting again when Mina finally tugged on my arm.

"Come on, I'll take you back home."

My little sister still lived at home. Rather, she lived at home again after staying in the college dorms didn't work out for her. I glanced at Mina for a minute, and decided her problems would be a good way to avoid my own.

"What ever happened between you and-"

"Don't say her name," Mina barked angrily.

"Okay, but what happened?" Mina had a good friend who had almost seemed like part of the family for a while and then suddenly, she stopped coming around and Mina was tight lipped about whatever caused their fall out.

"She just did something horrible that I never want to talk about again. Can we leave it at that?"

I nodded, though my eyes never left Mina as she ushered us to her car and helped me make sure I had every bit of my wedding gown inside before she shut the door. I wasn't sure how I managed to fit in her tiny little Mazda Miata, especially with all the extra fabric from the gown draped around me, but we somehow managed. Mina's choice in cars was something Flynn and I always teased her about.

"One day, you're going to have to upgrade your little toy car, Mina," I teased. She didn't even smile in response, just hopped in and got us on the road.

I had failed Mina as a big sister somehow. The knowledge made my heart ache even more than it had before. "Mina, if you ever want to talk about anything, you know I'm here. Right?"

Mina tipped her head up and down once but didn't bother responding. She focused instead on driving us out of Atlanta and to our parents' estate. My family was wealthy, which was why I didn't understand what Law's family always had against me. They treated me like I was the proverbial girl from the wrong side of the tracks. Maybe, it was my profession that made them see me as less than, but if that was it, I wouldn't apologize for it.

I was a language arts teacher at a middle school near where my apartment used to be located. I had been on the north side of Atlanta, in a smaller town on the outskirts, and didn't look forward to the commute through the city in order to live in Law's condo. It was one of the arguments I made for buying a house quickly rather than waiting like he wanted to.

In hindsight, I understood his hesitation. At least he did me a favor there. Except for the fact that I no longer had an apartment to call home. That was a giant pain in the butt. I would have to spend some of the money I'd squirreled away for a down payment on a house to find a new place to live.

"You could always stay with Flynn," Mina told me. I groaned when we pulled into the long driveway.

"Ew," was all I managed to say before both Mina and I burst into laughter. Our older brother, Flynn, was a confirmed bachelor and planned to stay that way for life if you asked him. There was nothing wrong with that, except it meant that his place had a revolving door for women and let's just say, my sister and I had both learned the hard way that our brother didn't keep his business to the bedroom.

"Yeah," Mina wrinkled her nose in disgust, obviously remembering the same lessons I had learned. "That wouldn't be a good idea at all."

"The last time I was over there, he offered me a seat on his couch, and I just couldn't. I was honestly worried about what I might catch from the thing," I joked.

Mina laughed harder as she parked the car in front of our parents' mansion. There really wasn't any other way to describe it. The place was sort of ostentatious, but it would always be home when I needed a place to land. Knowing you had a place to go when you were down on your luck was comforting. Actually, being down on your luck and left with no other option was a different story. Feeling like a failure was no fun, even if it wasn't my fault.

"I can't believe I had to come here after my wedding day," I lamented as we got out of the car.

"Could be worse, I guess." Mina said as she rounded the car and came to take hold of my hand.

"How so?"

She shrugged her shoulders. "I don't know. You could have married Law first and then found out about a torrid affair upon returning from your honeymoon with my future niece or nephew in your belly."

I gasped. "What is wrong with you?"

"I don't know. Maybe I read too much."

"What in the world kind of books are you reading? Maybe you need to find a new genre."

Mina laughed at my suggestion. "Nah. I'm good with the slap of ugly reality I get from darker romances. It stings less than being disappointed by fairytales that never come true."

Not for the first time, I wondered what happened to my baby sister to make her so anti-love. It also, once again, made me feel like I'd been a bad big sister and missed something important that she might have needed me for.

I glanced around the driveway and noticed all the other vehicles scattered about. "Great, everyone is here to witness my complete humiliation."

"Oh, come on!" My sister chimed in, sounding far too chipper. "They already saw that when you up and married an entirely different man at your wedding today."

She wasn't wrong about that, but it didn't detract from the fact that I now had to face everyone after making the decision to do just that. I was sure there would be lots of questions – ones I didn't particularly feel up to answering.

"Come on, my beautiful sister. The quicker we get this over with, the sooner you can go sulk in the soaker tub and try to drown your troubles in bubbles." Mina said this giddily as she clapped her hands together. My sister was a complete contradiction. She was always bubbly and happy, making everyone around her want to smile at her ridiculousness. Then, there was her darker, "love doesn't exist" side that was just so contrary. That side of her hadn't always been there. The fact that it was a recent addition to her personality, in the wake of her best friend no longer being present in her life, made me worry all the more. It was a concern for another day, though. She'd already made it clear that it wasn't a topic we would broach any time soon.

I allowed my sister to enter our family's home first, but it didn't take long before Mom was there with her arms wrapped around me. Granna was there before long too, enveloping me in her powder-fresh scent. She took my hands in her own and looked me in the eyes before pulling me closer so she could whisper in my ear.

"It might come with some challenges, but my ring rests on your finger tonight because one young man would stop at nothing to see you happy."

"If that's true, then where Is he?" I asked, knowing I was unable to hide the sadness in my voice.

My granna pulled back and winked at me. "He's been here all along, waiting for you to come home." I glanced around and when I didn't see any sign of Ky, she grinned at me knowingly. "He's out back with your brother and the rest of the men. I do believe they were trying to reassure him that you didn't run off on your honeymoon with Law after all."

"As if I would do that," I countered.

"Well, the heart is known to do crazy things sometimes. Take for instance," she patted the ring on my finger – the one that used to be hers – and smiled.

"I suppose you're right about that."

"Of course, I am, dear. Granna is always correct. If my Thomas were here today, he would tell you just that." We both laughed knowing good and well that my poppy would never have agreed to that. He would say, "Yes dear," to her face while vehemently denying it behind her back. She knew. He knew that she knew. It was their thing. I honestly wasn't sure how Granna was able to keep going without him by her side any longer.

"Go on, dear one, go put that boy out of his misery. He needs to know you're not upset with him after today."

I didn't understand why he would think that. We had already discussed things at the church earlier, but then I remembered the last moment I saw him and what Ky must have overheard. Hopefully, he didn't think a long-ago memory managed to resurrect the anger and hurt I'd felt as a heartbroken teenage girl.

I ignored my aunt and uncle's pinched face looks of disdain as I passed through the house and headed out the backdoor into the beautifully landscaped courtyard, complete with barbecue pit that could rival most high-end kitchens, pool, lounge area, and the huge outdoor table my mom had commissioned. The thing could seat twenty people easily. A long length of it was backed by an eight-foot hedge row and faced the pool while the other side faced whoever happened to be sitting across from them. Needless to say, I always chose to sit with my back to the hedge.

Kylan sat at the backside of the pool, nearest the very far end of the table, with his bare feet dipped into the water. My brother sat beside him, both of them with a beer in hand. I'd have to remember to thank Flynn for being there for Ky when I couldn't be. They had never been friends growing up because of the age difference, but as we all came into adulthood, and age stopped distancing us so much, the two of them had formed a closer friendship over the years.

When Flynn glanced up and saw me approaching, he stood and offered to take Ky's empty as I removed my shoes and hiked up my dress so I could sit down and dip my own aching feet into the water.

"Crazy day, huh?" I finally managed to say.

"I guess you could say that." Ky mumbled back, still averting his eyes from me as he seemingly watched the water ripple thanks to our disturbance. We sat that way in silence for a bit before he asked his question. "Why didn't you ever tell me?"

For a moment, I thought to feign ignorance, but I respected Ky too much to make him spell it out for me. Instead, I sighed and volleyed back, "Why would I?"

He turned to me then. "Seriously? Because we were best friends."

"Yes, and your actions made it clear that's all we were – to you. If I had told you, and you didn't feel the same, it could have been the end of our friendship."

"It nearly ended anyway, remember?" He asked. I nodded my head because it was true, especially after I turned him down for prom and he got angry with me. "I asked you to prom," he reminded me, as if he knew exactly what I'd been thinking.

"Yes, and I didn't want to go to prom as your pity date."

"My pity date?" His shock over my statement was odd.

"No one else asked me. I thought, after I saw you with Olivia, that you were only asking because no one else had done so. Olivia had already bragged to the other girls that she was going with you and that the two of you were a couple."

"We were not," he denied vehemently.

"You forget that I saw you with her – intimately."

Ky sighed and ducked his head into his hands. "It wasn't

like that. Jesus, you're going to think I'm stupid when I tell you," He insisted.

"I'm listening. Tell me."

"I was nervous. You had never been kissed, never even dated yet. I wanted to be your first everything," Ky admitted. That threw me for a total loop, considering what I'd walked in on back then.

"What? But…" I started to question, and remind him that I'd seen him with someone else, but he brought his hand up in a gesture meant to quiet me. So, I waited.

"Bea, I mean it. Nervous was an understatement. I couldn't screw up your first time and have you forever remember me as the awful way you lost your virginity. So, stupidity won out. Everyone knew Olivia was experienced because all the guys talked about her. I thought I could, you know, learn a few things. That way, when I was with you," he shrugged his shoulders looking incredibly sheepish as he admitted this to me. "At least then, I'd know what to do so I wouldn't hurt you or make it awful. I never realized that you saw me with her," he confided as I sat there in stunned silence.

"I didn't mean for things to go as far as they did with Olivia that day. Honestly, I never meant to actually have sex with her at all, but then one thing led to another and the next thing I knew, she put me inside of her. If that's what you saw, then it had to be the absolute worst timing in the history of bad timing because I blew in less than a minute, shoved her off me, and yelled at her for doing that. You and I were supposed to have that experience together, Bea. It was never supposed to be Olivia. She was only supposed to teach me some other stuff, but she stole that from me – from us. Granted, I put her in the position to take it, but that was never my intention."

I sat quietly, trying to digest everything he was saying. Taking my silence as him needing to keep going, I continued to listen as he spoke again.

"I refused to speak to Olivia after that because even though I was an asshole for using her the way I did, to learn about some things, she took something from me that I couldn't get back. If she was spreading rumors about us being together, they were lies."

If I thought my mind had been blown earlier when my fiancé left me a note, or later when he showed up to watch me marry someone else, it didn't compare to learning this. Everything I thought I knew in high school about my best friend was suddenly being painted in a different light.

"I asked you to prom and you told me that you already had a date," he reminded me.

"I lied."

He nodded his head, as if he already knew as much. "I couldn't figure out who would have been stupid enough to ask you out because I'd already told everyone that you were mine."

"You did what?" I asked. His answer was only to bob his head in confirmation. Then we both sat quietly for a moment before I needed further explanation. "I don't understand, Ky."

"You turned me down, wouldn't tell me who you were going with, and no one would fess up to asking you. I was so angry and jealous. I didn't realize you thought I was really with Olivia the whole time. I just figured you weren't into me like that. When Olivia walked by, I just grabbed her and asked, in front of you, hoping you would tell me I was making a mistake."

We were such a mess when we were younger. I finally looked up and glanced around to see that everyone had gone inside and left us alone out by the pool. It was probably for the best since I couldn't seem to control the tears leaking from my eyes as Ky spoke again.

"At prom, I kept watching for you. Olivia was pissed because I ignored her the whole time and just waited to see you walk through those doors. After the first two hours, when I still didn't see you there with a date or your friends, I got worried. I called your house, and your mom told me you were sick and couldn't go. I offered to come check on you, but she said you wouldn't want that."

"No, I wouldn't have," I admitted, "because I was at home crying in the prom dress my mom had bought for me. She thought for sure I was supposed to go with you and when I told her that you had a date, I think she might have been just as heartbroken as I was." It was true. My mom had been devastated for me. It was the first time I had really ever talked to her about my feelings for Ky.

"When I went back to school on Monday, I heard all about your prom, the hotel excursion, and had to watch you parade Olivia around on your arms for two weeks while you ignored me," I reminded Ky. "She laughed in my face because she was the one to break our 'unbreakable friendship'," I admitted to him.

Ky's head snapped around, so he was facing me then. "She did what?"

I laughed. "Come on, you had to know," I accused. "It was a challenge for most of the girls in our school. As you went through one after another, they all came back and told me everything you did with them – to them." He flinched at that, eyes wide and sorrow-filled. "Why did you think I never spoke to you again until we ran into one another at the beach at the end of summer?"

He swallowed and then angrily swiped at the tears that ran down his own face. "I went out with Julie after Olivia because she told me about seeing you and Greg at the movies making out."

I laughed once more. "I never dated or went out with anyone in high school." Ky's puzzled look made me wonder how my best friend and I had ever gotten so far off course with one another. "It took me until college, after seeing you with all those other girls, for me to get over losing you that way. I knew that it had all just been some fantasy I had concocted because I crushed on my best friend when I shouldn't have, but it still stung every time those girls threw it in my face.

"As we became friends again that summer, and all through senior year, I let each of your dates and new girl-friends harden my heart and serve as a reminder that you didn't see me like that. I was just a friend. Only ever your friend. Even as I told myself that, I couldn't bring myself to date anyone else."

"But you went to senior prom at another school, with some asshole who went there."

"No, Ky, I didn't go to any prom." His jaw literally dropped. "I didn't even tell you that lie either, so don't get mad at me. Some other girl did, so that you would take her. I guess she was afraid you would ask me for some reason."

"Because that was my plan until I found out you were

going to another school's prom that same night." He seemed completely baffled. "Where were you then?"

"Here," I told him honestly as I spread my hands in front of me, indicating the house where I'd grown up.

"Why, Bea? All you ever talked about during Freshman and Sophomore years was what prom was going to be like, what you were going to wear, and how breathtaking it was going to be."

"No one ever asked me." I shrugged my shoulders and looked away as he continued to stare.

"You never attended a single prom, anywhere?"

I shook my head.

"It's all my fault," he whispered. Part of me wanted him to take on that blame, but I made my own choices. I chose to stay home because I couldn't stomach seeing him happy and dancing with some other girl while all dressed up. My early dreams of prom had always included my best friend as my date. It was bad enough having to see him in the hallways and at lunch carrying on with them. I couldn't go and watch as they got to live out my prom dream while I sat on the sidelines with a broken heart.

"I warned all the guys away, two years in a row, and then…" He scrubbed his hands down his face and made some weird noise of distress. "You shouldn't marry me for real. I had no idea I'd screwed up so badly and cost you so much back then, Bea. I'm so sorry."

"We were kids, Ky. Neither one of us was great at communicating. My mom used to tell me that the hormones were the devil, and they made it harder for boys and girls to be friends at that age because we couldn't figure out how to talk anymore. Back then, I thought she was just making excuses to ease my broken heart. With age comes wisdom though, and looking back, I know she was right."

"Gotta say, I wish she had been wrong."

"I don't." It was the honest truth.

"What the hell does that mean?"

"Ky, we were both far too immature then, obviously, considering the massive miscommunications and stupid decisions that we both made. Imagine if we had tried to date, especially with all those girls constantly trying to break us up. We would have never made it and might not even be friends now as a result. Then who would have been there to save me from the crappiest day ever?" I ruffled the silk sheath dress I wore to get married in in order to highlight my point.

"Or maybe we'd already be married – legally – with two kids and a dog," he suggested.

"Are you kidding? You were so easily led astray from me by Olivia, Julia, and all the others. There's no way we would have made it back then." My best friend offered a dubious look of disbelief that I just shrugged it off. Knowing the truth was something completely different than being able to let go of old hurts. I had spent enough time living in denial that going back to that place wasn't somewhere I wanted to be.

"What about now?" He asked. "Is there a chance for us now?"

I smiled at him. "As of this morning, when I woke up, I was still in a relationship with someone else," I reminded him.

"Yes, but we've been in our own crazy relationship for fifteen years. I think that means something."

"It does. That's the only reason I would even entertain dating someone else right now."

"Dating? Just dating?" He asked as he reached down and spun his grandfather's ring that sat on his finger. "Does that mean you don't want to make what we did today official?"

That was a difficult question to answer. I actually wished it was already official and that our spur of the moment choice earlier today meant more than it did. I'd never take it back. Knowing we had a choice though, gave me pause to wonder if we'd done the right thing. "I'm torn," I finally answered as honestly as I could.

"Because you still want to marry Law?"

It was a fair question, but I shook my head as I answered. "I told Law earlier that I couldn't marry him now. The trust we had is completely broken." Plus, there was that nagging reminder in the back of my mind that I felt relieved. I had also been humiliated and angry, but what I didn't feel at all today – where Law was concerned – was devastated. Destroyed. Ruined. All things I probably should have felt at being stood up on my wedding day. It just wasn't there.

"Do you wish you'd married him today as planned?"

"No. I'm glad it never happened." I owed it to Ky to be completely honest with him, but I also owed it to myself to acknowledge what I'd just said. If I had never received that letter from Law today, I would have gone through with it, and most likely ended up with a failed marriage as a result. My head was in it, but my heart, she had been sitting stagnant for quite some time. Sure, I loved Law in a way, but I never had that mad, passionate in-love with him feeling.

Weren't you supposed to experience that with the person you were meant to be with?

Ky grinned at me. "Good. So, do you want to maybe go on a date with me tomorrow?"

I laughed at Ky's timing and the boyish grin that accompanied his question. "I would love to."

"Okay then." His hand still fiddled with the ring on his finger. "I won't take it off, Bea." He finally said to me, as if confessing a dark secret. "I need you to know that I can't do that. Our marriage might not be legal just yet, but I made promises to you, our families, and myself before God, and I plan to honor them, no matter what the law has to say about it."

Tears pooled in my eyes at his admission. "I take it seriously too, Ky." He let out a huge breath, as if he'd been holding it while awaiting my response. "I know we made vows to one another, and that we've been in one another's lives forever," I started to say.

"But?"

"This is a new journey for us and I had a different fiancé this morning, so I want to take things slow. We know one another as best friends. Bea and Ky. We need to get to know one another as something more now."

"Whatever you need, we'll work on it. I only have one request."

"What's that?"

"I know that Law isn't going to let this go easily, despite his cowardly note and trying to jump ship first. It was one thing for him to be the one letting go of your relationship. It's another for him to think he's been made a fool of. So, I need you to be honest with me when it comes to him. If you're talking to him, meeting with him, or if your feelings compel you to be with him again... Please, let me know first."

"Of course." There was no way I could even think of being with Law again, but I understood Ky's worry. It was a legitimate one. That's why I'd held onto Law's letter. It was the one thing I could hold onto that was tangible. It was like a talisman, there to remind me of my anger, of his betrayal, and ultimate cowardice. I needed that because no matter what, spending more than two years with someone left you with a familiarity that was hard to break.

Chapter Nine

BEA

"I'VE NEVER BEEN HERE," I mentioned as we walked into the restaurant while Ky held my hand.

Ky said something to the hostess and then turned to me with an odd look in his eyes. "You've never been here for dinner before?"

"Nope. I always wanted to come, but…" I let the words trail off. Law would never bring me. He said it wasn't the best place to go on dates because it could be too loud, and the atmosphere was all wrong. Looking around the place, I knew he lied, and it made me wonder why. What in the world could he have been hiding that he never wanted me to come here?

"Well, good. Then you get to experience it with me first." Ky grinned as he said it, and I couldn't help the petty little voice in the back of my mind that reminded me that he had obviously been here before, and it wasn't with me. Ugh! I had to stop. That wasn't fair to him. We weren't together then. I refused to let my issues with Law cloud my experience with Ky. Darn it.

We were seated not far from the bar and Ky seemed almost embarrassed by that. "What's wrong?"

His cheeks were a little pink. "This was the best seat I could get without a reservation, but it will probably end up a little loud, rather than romantic."

I glanced around and noticed that the seats further away, near the windows, had candlelit tables and seemed a bit quainter than the one we were seated at. The candle wasn't even present at our table, and he was right, there were a bunch of men sitting at the bar. While a quick glance showed me they were all in business suits and seemed like upscale clientele, that didn't stop them from dissolving into frat-bro talks about banging their secretaries.

"You just wanted to slide up between your secretary's double-Ds. It's different for me." The speaker coughed and cleared his throat, clearly either having been sick or something recently.

Still, the voice sounded oddly familiar. Despite my curiosity, I chose to ignore the noise around us so that Ky wouldn't feel worse about our seating arrangements.

"You dodged a fucking bullet, if you ask me." Another recognizable voice said from amongst the suit-wearing frat-bros. Why did that voice raise my hackles?

"He's right. Think about it, now you can go get all the pussy you want without having to hear some woman nagging at you when you get home about how your suit smells funny."

"Your wife wouldn't nag about that shit if you didn't smell like every brand of perfume she doesn't wear when you come home, asswipe!" That familiar voice said again.

"Where is Jackie? I miss being able to watch her walk

into the room," one of the men mentioned. It tickled something at the back of my mind, the familiar voices, that name...

"Blame *him* for that. He had to tell Jackie all about his feelings on his fucking wedding day and scared her away." I turned to see Todd, my ex-fiancé's best friend standing there glancing out at the rest of the restaurant. He appeared to be looking for someone, but that ended when his eyes locked with mine. His ears went red and I knew in that instant I was the bullet he was telling someone they dodged, which meant...

"Shit! Do you think she heard me?" Todd asked one of the men as they all sat at the bar waiting to see what I might do if I had indeed heard him.

I turned my head slowly and watched as Todd tapped someone on the shoulder and then pointed in my direction. There he was. My fiancé. Ex-fiancé.

That reminded me, I really needed to give him his ring back. It occurred to me what else Todd had just divulged. Jackie was usually here. He scared her away with his feelings. Oh wow! Jackie was the woman from Law's letter. My heart sank because I had been her friend, and I thought she had also been mine.

Law didn't seem to notice my distress, or realize I'd just overheard those things, as he stumbled off his barstool and headed in our direction. Ky finally noticed that my attention had stayed on the men at the bar a bit too long and swiveled around to see what I was so focused on.

"Shit! You have got to be kidding me."

"He would never take me here," I mentioned as Law nearly knocked over a waitress who was in his way. She wouldn't have been, if he had been able to walk a straight line. "Now, I know why."

"Why?" Ky asked in a worried tone.

"They just mentioned Jackie. She's not here this time because *someone* told her all about his feelings for her."

Ky nodded, as if it wasn't news to him. Maybe it wasn't. He had questioned why I'd invited her to the movies with us a couple weeks back. I liked her. We had hit it off at one of Law's work functions and had been friends ever since. I wasn't sure how she felt about Law, but knowing that he had feelings for her that were strong enough to make him walk away from our relationship on our wedding day made me rethink exactly how close the two had been.

Ky waived our waiter away quickly and told him to give us a few minutes as Law finally made it into our space. I didn't think we would need those minutes though because I didn't feel up to sticking around after seeing my ex-fiancé and all his work mates. They all knew he left me on our wedding day to tell their other coworker all about his feelings for her. It seemed my humiliation, thanks to Law's selfishness, was never to end.

"Fancy seeing you here," Law spat out, and honestly I was surprised that his words hadn't been slurred terribly. They were somewhat sluggish on delivery.

"Yes, fancy seeing *me* here, since you refused to bring me to this place, even though I asked repeatedly. Imagine how it must feel for me to find out exactly why you never brought me here. This is where you came with your other woman," I accused.

"Damn. Is that about Jackie?" One of the men asked,

though Law seemed oblivious. Ky's eyes shifted from Law to mine.

"What are you doing here?" Law asked, seemingly oblivious to everything. "You broke me and now you're out to eat with him? At *my* place?"

"I think that's about enough," Ky told him.

"Yeah, it really is," Law agreed. "So, are you coming home tonight or what?"

Ky stiffened and while he appeared to be ignoring Law, he was staring right at me. "You left your stuff, and you haven't come back for it, so you're thinking about things, right?" Law asked.

I continued to keep my eyes on Ky, not Law, as I shook my head. Law didn't seem to notice the head shake and poked my shoulder when he didn't get a response he could process.

"*Your* condo is not *my* home."

"It is. You moved all your things in."

"Yes, and you let me do that knowing that you had another woman in the picture. Then, you left me on our wedding day to go be with her. Sorry about your bad luck that she turned you down."

"Come on, I 'pologized for that." Law swayed as if a breeze attempted to push him over, but it was just whatever alcohol he had consumed, catching up with him.

"Law, go sit down," I demanded.

"Not until you tell me you're coming home."

My head hurt. It was interesting to note that my heart did not. Knowing Law, and his crush on another woman, was the reason I'd never been able to come here, and now that he was ruining my night out with Ky - our first date, all

I wanted was to go home. Not to Law's condo. Just not here. I stood and grabbed my things then turned to Ky.

"Can we go?"

He stood too, because the man was a saint. He threw a twenty down on the table even though we hadn't even been able to order a drink yet.

"You're gonna leave? Just like that?"

"You're drunk. Go home Law. Get yourself together and figure out what you want out of life."

He grabbed my arm to stop me from walking away. "I want you. Dammit, I already told you that I want you to come home."

"You should have decided that sooner. That isn't an option you even get to hope for anymore because I no longer want you."

Ky reached over and pushed Law's hand off my arm and then moved me to his other side. With his hand on my lower back, he guided me out of the restaurant.

"I can't believe that just happened."

"What did he mean in there? It sounded like you had a conversation where you agreed to keep your stuff at his place until you decided what to do."

"When you left the church and he was still there, he begged me to leave my stuff and give everything some time and thought before deciding my next step. I didn't agree to do that, but I also didn't go pick my stuff up right away. I figured everyone could use some time to cool down first before a bunch of drama started from me trying to reclaim my life." I threw my hand toward the restaurant. "Apparently, the drama was meant to find me anyway."

"I'm sorry," Ky's apology felt wrong.

"For what?"

"Bringing you here."

"Did you know he would be here?" Ky shook his head. "Then what are you apologizing for? That scene wasn't your fault. I should be the one saying I'm sorry because my drama ruined our first date."

Ky stopped me before we managed to get to his vehicle. His hands found my hips and pulled enough that it became an invitation, and not a demand for me to move closer to him. When I went with the motion and closed the space between us, he leaned in and placed a peck of a kiss right on the tip of my nose.

"You ruined nothing, Sweet Bea." I grinned at the nickname he'd given me years ago. He hadn't used it in forever. Once, when we were a whole lot younger, Ky heard my mom calling me sweet pea, but he thought she said sweet Bea, so he started calling me that. When he realized he'd just heard her wrong, he refused to stop, saying, *'It's my thing now'*. After that, my mom wouldn't call me sweet pea anymore. She went with sweetie or sweetheart instead.

"You want to try somewhere else?"

"How about we just pick something up and head back to my place so we don't stand a chance of running into anyone else who might want to rehash things?" He hung his head a little as he assisted me into his car. "It was poor timing to suggest our first date out this soon, anyway. We'll make up for it soon."

"You are wise beyond your years," I teased. "I'm not upset about the timing, though, Ky. Everything would have been fine if we hadn't accidentally walked into *his* place." I rolled my eyes at the thought. The jerk went there enough to lay claim to it, but he refused to ever take me and he thought I'd agree to go back to him after everything else and then that, too? Yeah, he must have been drunker than he appeared.

AFTER WE PICKED UP TAKEOUT, we ate in relative quiet before moving to his bedroom to get comfy and watch a movie. That was nothing out of the ordinary for the two of us. Ky had a great system set up in his bedroom versus the living room because he used to have a roommate who would constantly hog the TV. After his roommate moved out, and Ky decided to keep the place for himself, he never bothered to move everything back out to the living room.

He handed me one of his shirts and a pair of basketball shorts that I had to tie and roll down at the top to get a decent fit. Even after the adjustments, they were still uncomfortable to wear while lying on a bed, so I took them off, thinking the t-shirt came almost to mid-thigh anyway. Ky never said a word because that wasn't exactly out of the realm of normal for us. I'd borrowed his clothes more times than I could count over the years.

As we laid there watching an action movie, I played with the ring that now circled my finger. I'd like to say it was an absent gesture, but honestly, I knew what I was doing. My granna had offered her ring to me when she found out I was engaged to Law, though he had been with me when it happened, and had refused on my behalf before I could say a word. It had angered me then, and we'd even fought about it later that night. My granna never said a word about it after that, but she also never spoke to Law again. He had been moved to the top of her 'poop-list' as she called it.

Thinking back to moments like that, I realized there had been red flags all along that I shouldn't have ignored in my relationship with Law. Another had been his refusal to take me to the restaurant I wanted to try so bad, and now I knew there had been a perfectly logical reason – on his part – for his refusal. That too had been a red flag I'd missed. My heart hurt just thinking about it. Oddly enough, not because I was broken up about the loss of Law, but because I allowed myself to stay with a man who couldn't be trusted to do right by me.

My phone rang and pulled me from my thoughts. I glanced at it to see Law's face pop on the screen. Ky watched me as I turned the thing off and then he reached over to his and followed suit before tucking them both onto the nightstand.

"Come on," he presented his chest with his arms wide open and there was no hesitation on my part before I slid into the warmth and comfort he offered.

I HAD STAYED at Ky's place many times over the years, and borrowed his clothes too. None of that was new. Waking up in his arms in the morning, with his front spooned up against my back – that was different. We had never slept all night in the same bed before. Either he had given up his bed for me or I had fallen asleep on the couch. My heart swelled and for just a moment, I let myself live in the bliss of a dream I'd once had when I was much younger.

Plenty of girls dreamed of going to bed with Kylan Armstrong. I was the one who always fantasized about waking up in his arms. Maybe it was my innocence, back when my crush on him had been at its height, but the sex part of a relationship with him had always been on the back burner of my mind.

It was the intimate moments I craved the most. The kisses we might one day share, having him hold me, and waking up in his arms had been the stuff of my dreams. Sure, there were the occasional dirty dreams too, but I wasn't ready to recall those just yet. Not while lying in bed beside him, half naked, and well, recently sort-of married. The last thought gave me pause.

We were married. Didn't that mean sex should be a given? It wasn't legal though, not until we signed the paperwork. Granted, it wasn't like I was waiting on marriage to have sex. I'd been with two other men. It's just that this was Ky, my Ky, and…

"If you think any harder over there, you're going to give me a headache," Ky mumbled into my hair before he planted a kiss on my head and rolled to his back. He never let go of me as he moved, so I was forced to follow his movements or cut off our connection. I wasn't ready for the latter, so I rolled with him and snuggled my front into his side while resting my head in that perfect little spot where his chest and arm met.

"Sorry," I muttered. "I was just running through my memories."

"About?" He asked, and I hadn't missed the way his body stiffened slightly beneath mine. The tension gave me pause, but only for a moment.

"This is the first time we've slept together."

Ky chuckled. "Yeah, not how I'd imagined we would end up snuggled together in the morning, but I'm not complaining either," he teased.

Sudden banging on his door startled both of us. Ky gently moved me to the side and slid out of the bed. "Be right back." He got up and stood there beside the bed, and stretched his muscles. My eyes refused to look away, no matter how many times I begged them to. Ky only wore a pair of shorts, and they hung on for dear life at the base of his hips, obviously having been pulled lower from his movements in his sleep. My eyes dipped from his muscular chest, down his glorious torso, and then my devilish orbs continued to follow his treasure trail of hair down to where his muscles dipped into a "v" that pointed to…

BANG. BANG. BANG

I glanced back up after the banging on the door startled me again to see that Ky grinned at me knowingly. He winked and took off to see who in the heck had attempted to tear his door down before ten in the morning.

Curious, I got up to follow him, in case it was someone in my family checking to see if I was alive. I forgot that we both turned our phones off the previous night, and I hadn't remembered to let my parents know that I wouldn't be coming home. It wasn't out of disrespect or thinking I was too old to have to be considerate. I simply hadn't lived with them in so long that it didn't occur to me that I needed to be considerate of anyone else by letting them know my whereabouts.

As soon as I rounded the corner into the hallway with a clear view of the front door, my stomach felt as though it dropped to my feet. Law stood there, looking angrier than he had a right to be. His eyes scanned my body, taking in the fact that I was wearing a t-shirt that obviously belonged to Ky. It wasn't lost on him that we both must have just come from the bedroom – from bed – considering our attire and rumpled appearances. Our half-dressed, mussed hair, sleepily contented faces all dug under Law's skin as his scowl deepened.

"I'm so easily replaced?" He asked me with a low, menacing voice. Ky moved to step into his line of sight, effectively blocking me from view, but I managed to move closer. I put a hand on Ky's lower back to let him know I was okay, and he slid the slightest bit to the right so that I could face Law, even as his body blocked enough of me that I would be safe from attack. Not that Law would ever put his hands on me, but the gesture wasn't' missed by anyone.

"No easier than you replaced me on our wedding day. How would that look right now if she hadn't shut you down? Would you even care where I spent my night? Would I be the one standing on your doorstep while the other woman – Jackie was it? – stood there in your shirt?"

Law staggered back as if I struck him. "It wouldn't have been like that. I would have been respectful."

Ky scoffed as his muscles bunched with the tension from holding himself still. "About as respectful as you leaving your fiancé a note about going to woo another woman on your wedding day?" He asked before his anger got the better of him. "Get out of here with your judgment. Bea fell asleep at my place, watching a movie, because we are being respectful of one another. You didn't factor into that equation at all. Why should you?" He made a tsking sound at Law then.

"Don't preach to Bea about being disrespectful just because you feel like things turned around on you. It was your disrespect of her that set everything in motion."

I was shocked that Ky didn't attempt to insinuate more happened between us just to get under Law's skin. My respect for my best friend rose just a bit higher in the wake of his words.

"Well, obviously Bea wasn't serious about marrying you then, if you can't even seal the deal with her." Law showed his true colors as he sniped back at Ky. Then he turned his attention toward me alone. "I promise, I will prove to you that we're meant to be together, Bea. I'll work to fix things and then we'll say our vows to one another the way we were supposed to."

I wanted to laugh, but honestly I was speechless. He literally stood there and told me that if Jackie had said yes, he would have been respectful during the shift from being with me to his new woman. Then suddenly he changed gears and told me we belong together, and the idiot didn't see the problem with that at all.

"Vows don't seem to be something you're capable of making," Ky explained to my ex-fiancé when I couldn't find the words to respond. Then, Ky slammed the door shut in Law's face and turned to pull me into his arms. My failure to return the gesture right away worried my best friend enough that he pulled away and looked me in the eye. "Are you angry with me for saying that?"

"No, he deserved far more than your parting shot — which was just you speaking the truth anyway." I leaned in then and wrapped my arms around his neck. "Thank you for keeping it classy and real earlier." I told Ky before sliding up to kiss his lips. It was a brief kiss, but so darn profound all at once. "He didn't deserve to know that we hadn't been together, but I appreciate you telling the truth on my behalf."

"If you're going to reward me with kisses, then I can't wait to be honest again," he teased. Though judging from the heated look in his eyes he meant every word.

I laughed and thought maybe it would end there and we could move on to breakfast and being our normal selves, but I was quickly disavowed of those notions.

"Really," Ky told me as his fingers slipped under my chin to lift my face so that our eyes met once more. "My shirt looks sexy as hell on you, Bea." He puckered up, as if that bit of 'honesty' deserved a reward. I gently face-palmed him and playfully pushed him away. Then quickly spun on my heels and made my way back to his room so that I could get dressed. Ky followed me, as he pouted about not getting another kiss.

"Your ass looked fantastic in those jeans last night." Ky told me as I bent to retrieve them from the floor. "But I might prefer this view way more." I turned to see his head tilted slightly as his eyes remained glued to my ass. The t-shirt I wore rode up in the back, as I bent and he could probably see my upper thighs and a little panty-clad ass cheek before I rose back up with jeans in hand.

I couldn't hide the grin while turning fully to face Ky who had stepped closer to land us toe-to-toe. He deserved a kiss for more honesty. There was no reason to deny that I wanted to reward him. My best friend -pseudo husband- had driven me to the brink of insanity with his never-ending comments and the sexy smolder that threatened to light fire to my panties. I leaned in and nibbled on his top lip, leaving the plumper bottom one alone for now. This too had been a dream of mine long ago, and the reality didn't disappoint.

As I kissed him, Ky reached out and pulled my body forward, bringing us so close that his body's reaction made it perfectly clear how he felt in that moment. The proof of it was plastered against my torso. Instead of the playful little nibble I meant to leave him with, Ky deepened the kiss while stealing my very breath from me. He then made me a promise with his mouth that he was being honest with me once more – just not in words this time.

Chapter Ten

BEA

I'D LIKE to say that our steamy kiss ended in the consummation of our marriage, but another knock on Ky's door made certain we weren't going to be able to finish what we started, at least not yet. It was for the best anyway because in all honesty, I still had a lot to think about. Whether our nuptials should be legalized was at the top of that list.

"It's probably Mina or Flynn coming to check on me for my parents. We should really turn our phones back on," I told Ky as he reluctantly released me.

"Maybe we should tape a 'do not disturb' note to the door for the day." My smile was answered with another, though much quicker, kiss. "Hold that thought while I go to reassure your family, and whatever you do, don't put those jeans back on." He grinned wickedly at me as he snatched the garment from my hands and took them with him to go answer the door. I ran after him, because there was no way I wanted to have a discussion with my brother – if that's who was knocking – while not wearing any pants.

"She's alive and well," Ky offered good naturedly as he answered the door. Unfortunately for him – and maybe me too - it was not my family on the other side of the door. Nope. It was a woman. She was tall, slender, and made up like she was about to walk a runway. That is, if that runway had a pole on the end of it, since her clothes were sorely missing. To be fair, she was wearing clothes, there just wasn't much of them to speak of. Her skirt would have looked like a chunky belt on me if I could have even managed to clasp it around my larger waistline. The shirt, well, the bottom half of her boobs were hanging out, so no further explanation needed there.

Ky stood speechless with the door gaping wide open. The woman's lips were frozen into a surprised "O". Then, very recognizable male laughter rang out from somewhere down the hallway, but not far enough away that we hadn't heard.

"Looks like you were so important to your new husband that he forgot to cancel his latest booty call," Law shouted. It was disturbing that he hadn't left yet. It was even more disturbing that the butt-wipe was partially correct.

"Um, what?" The woman asked as she turned her attention to Law for a moment and then back to Ky again. That time, she glanced down at his hand and noticed the ring sitting on a very prominent finger.

"Oh my God! Kylan! You got married?" Her lips poked out in a brief pout when he didn't respond. Then she popped a hip out and I had no doubt that Law, where he was seated a few feet away, got a great view of her naked ass thanks to the shift in the barely-there fabric. "What happened to 'I never do serious'?"

Ky finally snapped out of his shocked stupor and laughed. "If I recall correctly, I told you that I only do serious with one woman, and she wasn't you."

"So, you cheated on her with me all this time?"

"You and I hooked up twice, and never at my apartment, so I don't know why you're even here."

"He never cheated on me," I called out from over Ky's shoulder because I wouldn't have his good name besmirched. Okay, well, his slightly tarnished name shouldn't become full-on rusty at any rate.

I snagged my jeans and patted Ky on the shoulder. "I'm going to let you handle this while I go get dressed and call my family."

"I'm married," I heard him announce proudly. "Sandra, meet Law over there. He left my wife at the altar the other day – so I was the lucky bastard who got to marry her instead. You should hook up, since the woman he left that divine angel for turned him down." I stood there, three feet away from the door, with my jaw gaped open, and watched as Ky shut the door once more. That time, he made sure to throw all the locks, too.

"I think the 'do not disturb' sign might be a necessity." He muttered before turning and realizing that I was still standing there. "I'm so sorry about that. She just showed up, and it wasn't like a planned hookup that I forgot to cancel or something. I don't even know how she got my address because she's never been here before."

I believed Ky because he didn't often bring women back to his place. He said it gave them the wrong idea and led to some wanting to overstay their welcome. It made me wonder if Law had something to do with Sandra showing up, and then that just led to more questions, like how he would know to contact her. None of it mattered anyway.

"You have nothing to apologize for," I reassured Ky. Then my stomach growled. Despite getting takeout from a Thai place on the way home the night before I hadn't eaten much of it and the lack of food was starting to catch up to me.

"Let's get dressed and go grab some breakfast," Ky offered.

THANKFULLY, when we made our way to breakfast, Law was no longer outside of Ky's house. Maybe he had left with Sandra after all. It probably should have stung to think about, but it didn't.

"What's wrong?" Ky asked.

"Honestly?"

"I will always prefer honesty, even if it hurts."

I nodded because the feeling was mutual. "I was wondering if Law and Sandra left together, but then I realized it didn't bother me." His brows crinkled down as he frowned at me. "Shouldn't I feel something? Isn't there supposed to be pain, heartbreak, anything at the thought of him leaving with another woman?"

"Maybe you're just in shock," Ky offered helpfully, though it seemed to pain him to do so.

I shook my head. "No. I'm not in shock; I just don't care. That made me disappointed in myself because it meant I never should have agreed to go through with marrying him anyway. "I was having my own doubts just before Todd showed up with that letter," I admitted.

"You were?" That seemed to surprise Ky.

"I was. It just didn't feel right. Then, of course, after I received the letter I chalked it up to my gut knowing what was coming but I think it was more than that. No, I know it was more than that because the thing that excited me the most about the wedding was buying all those tulips out of spite after Law's mother said only trash would have tulips for a wedding flower."

Ky laughed at that. "So, you got off on the pettiness of creating something his family would hate?"

"He hated it, too. Thank you, by the way."

"For what?"

"For wearing the tulip on your lapel yesterday."

"I wouldn't have worn anything else, Sweet Bea. They're your favorite."

Chapter Eleven

KY

"My place is closer to your work," I tossed out as Bea took her last bite of French toast. Her tongue poked out and dragged across her lips to swipe away any remaining syrup and I couldn't look away even if I was ordered to at gunpoint.

"Yes, I know where you live."

"It's closer than your family's place too. Since all your stuff was at Law's, I'm guessing you never resigned your lease."

"That is true." She placed her fork down on her plate and started to stack all the dishes in a nice pile at the edge of the table. Bea had worked as a waitress during college, even though her parents footed the bill for her tuition. She wanted to make them proud and pay for her own living expenses. Her family was always shocked to see her tidy everything, but I thought it was endearing. Having done the job, she wanted to make someone else's day a little easier whenever she ate at a restaurant.

"Okay, I'm not sure if you're dropping a hint or just spitting facts out at me, Kylan."

I clutched my hand over my heart. "Not the full name!" I widened my eyes dramatically as Bea giggled. "I know you want to go back to your family's place tonight so that you have the time to think about what to do tomorrow with the whole make it legal or let it go as an impulsive decision that ultimately had no consequences. The thing is, even if you decide not to marry me, you still need a place to live."

"So, you're saying even if we don't make it official, you're still willing to live in sin with me?" Her teasing tone made me want to flip her over my knees and spank her beautiful ass, but that wasn't something people were supposed to do while sitting in a pancake house just before noon on a Sunday when the church crowd had already started to trickle in.

"I'm being serious. Even if..." I hesitated because this was the part I didn't want to say out loud. "Even if you don't want to be in a relationship with me, other than friendship, my door is still open. We'll just have to agree on one major rule."

"What's that?"

"No bringing anyone else home. No offense, Bea, because I will always respect your decisions, but I don't think I could handle seeing you with anyone else."

She stared at me for a while and then nodded her head. "I know that feeling all too well, Ky."

Fuck. After hearing about how the girls I'd dated through high school had treated her without me knowing, it felt fucking insensitive as hell for me to tell her that I couldn't handle it when she had done so with more grace than I ever knew.

"Bea," I started but she stopped me with a shake of her head. Those beautiful raven curls of her bounced as she did.

"Let's just take it one step at a time and see what kind of clarity a good night's sleep, and a few hours apart, brings to each of us. This is a huge change for you as well. I need you to really think about how making everything official, or simply living together, dating, or whatever we mutually decide on will impact your life."

I grinned at her. "Already thought of all the angles, Sweet Bea. Been thinking of them since about middle school when you first started growing boobs."

She rolled her eyes, threw her napkin at me, and I wanted nothing more than to lean across the table and take her sweet lips in a heated kiss. I gave myself thirty seconds to decide and then dove in for that kiss anyway. My girl needed to know that I was done putting us on the back burner for idiotic reasons. Law was right about one thing; I was dumb as shit for not making it happen sooner.

Even if Bea had a point about how we were probably lucky we didn't try to get together back in high school, I knew deep down in my heart that I should have never backed down when she first met Law. I should have told her then and there that she'd never see the fucker again because she was going out with me.

Chapter Twelve

BEA

Lying in bed at my parents' house, I felt my phone vibrate beside me.

> Ky: Are you sure you don't want to come back?

> Bea: I will see you in the morning, promise.

> Ky: But my bed is really lonely without you.

> Bea: You know why I came here for the night.

> Ky: I still think you could think good thoughts about me from the comfort of my bed.

> Bea: You're unbelievable.

> Ky: And don't you forget it. 😉

How could I? The man was unforgettable as far as I was concerned. He always had been. While wrestling with how being married to him for real would affect our friendship, I had never once thought of being married to him as a bad thing. It had once been a dream of mine. It was a dream of mine again as I fell asleep that night full of nervous optimism.

This future might not have been my most recent plan, but it wasn't exactly a new idea either. That was the thing that I kept going back to in my mind. We weren't doing anything that either of us hadn't thought of doing before. Granted, I never knew Ky felt the same way I did previously, but finding out certainly helped me make my decision.

I was going to meet him in the morning to go to the courthouse and make everything official. We already walked down the aisle, all that was left was for us to make this new chapter of our lives work. Considering we both now knew that communication failures had been needlessly keeping us apart for years, it was a roadblock we hopefully wouldn't have to deal with moving forward.

Tomorrow, I would officially become Mrs. Beatrice Armstrong.

"Beatrice Armstrong." Goosebumps erupted across my arms as the name whispered from my lips. Disbelief marred the words, but then I said it again, and it just sounded so right. Ky was always meant to be mine.

My mind was made up. For better or worse, just like the vows we took on Friday, I was going to sign those papers, and we were going to make this marriage work.

"GOOD MORNING," Kylan said as soon as I opened the door for him on Monday.

"Morning." I yawned as I turned back around and headed for the kitchen. "Need coffee first."

Ky chuckled as he followed behind. "If you had woken up at my place, the coffee would have been ready for you."

"I'm glad I had the night to think things through."

"Did you reconsider?"

"No. That's just it. It was more like everything felt settled." I glanced back at Ky as I poured my coffee and added a little sweetener. "Does that seem weird?"

"No. It felt settled the day I watched you walk down the aisle toward me."

My heart stuttered in my chest as my eyes flew up to meet his. Ky's beautiful smile formed tiny little lines at the corners of his eyes which proved he was being genuine. "What?" He asked.

"It's a bit strange to hear you speak so candidly of feeling settled with me. I supposed, since I gave up on anything ever happening between us so long ago, it feels a bit shocking to hear you admit things like that."

"I guess I'll have to keep it up then. One day, you'll say it back without hesitation because it will feel normal, and no longer shocking. This is real for me, Bea. I know it feels like a hundred miles per hour toward a future that only felt like a dream at times, but it is real."

"I guess we better go make sure this marriage is legal then."

Ky leaned toward me and gently brushed his lips against mine. "I promise that you won't regret it."

"I appreciate that but I already know it in my heart. I trust you with my heart, Ky."

"Thank you for that, Sweet Bea. I won't let you down."

If only life was as simple as the promise my best friend made to me. Unfortunately, life was full of other factors that forced the best laid plans to be put on hold.

Case in point, the way the woman at the clerk of court's office stared at me as though I had two heads when we presented her with our paperwork from the pastor who married us, our birth certificate, picture IDs, and explained that we needed to apply for a license because we got married in a surprise ceremony.

"Ma'am, let me get this straight, you married this man?"

"Yes, my best friend, Kylan Armstrong."

"Uh-huh. But you had a marriage license to make things official with another man, Lawson Gregory, last week."

I nodded my head slowly. "Law left me at the altar with a note telling me that he was interested in another woman and he went to go try to make a go of it with her. While he was gone, my best friend stepped in and married me instead."

The woman's eyebrows hid somewhere in her hairline as her eyes rounded out in surprise. "Oh. Well, the thing is, Mr. Lawson Gregory was just here with a woman claiming to be Beatrice Robeson Gregory. They registered your marriage certificate not twenty minutes ago."

"Well, you're looking at my state issued driver's license, birth certificate, and my signature on the certificate Kylan and I signed with the pastor."

"No, you're right. It's obvious that you are Beatrice Robeson."

"How did another woman file a marriage certificate with you without proving her identity?"

"Well, we checked identity when the license was issued, and Mr. Gregory showed his ID, but they mentioned that they had to go back to the hotel where they honeymooned because his wife forgot her purse in the excitement to make things official this morning."

"That was very convenient of fake me to forget her purse."

"Obviously, fraud was committed, so you can just pull the certificate and void it out," Kylan suggested.

The woman bit her lip as her eyes shifted between us nervously. "I need to call the magistrate down for assistance with this. I do not have the power to alter records once they're officially placed."

"Even when you screwed up and allowed fraudulent records to be entered?" Ky growled his question at the woman. She flinched and took a step back just as a man came up behind her in the office.

"What's going on here, Bette?"

"Oh dear, it seems that I may have messed up." She went on to explain why Kylan and I were there and what happened with Law and the imposter woman coming in to file the paperwork. "I thought I remembered her. She had dark, curly hair. Not as curly as the real Ms. Robeson, but you know how people do different things with themselves." The poor lady shook as she handed over all the documentation to the man, who turned out to be the Magistrate Court Judge.

He sighed heavily and then turned his attention back up to us. "I'm sorry to say, folks, that Bette is right. She can't just remove the information on file. We have to go through the system to have that done."

"What exactly does that mean?"

"You will have to go through the process of having the marriage to Lawson Gregory officially annulled before we can remove the record."

"What? No!" I yelled. "We were never married. We never said vows to one another. I said them to Kylan when Law failed to show up for a wedding because he was chasing after another woman. How can you stand there and tell me that I'm now married to that asshole simply because he lied to this woman?"

"I'm so sorry. I know it isn't what you wanted to hear, but it is the only way to have the record wiped, and we will file criminal charges against Lawson and his accomplice." He leaned back and picked up the phone to call someone. "This is Judge Harrington. I need the surveillance video from the clerk of court's office for the past two hours and have the sheriff come to the clerk's office."

"If you two don't mind, it might help if you stick around and take a look at the footage. If you recognize the woman who came in with Lawson, it might speed up the process."

"I can't believe this is happening," I cried. Kylan wrapped his arm around me and pulled me tight to his side.

"It will be okay, Sweet Bea. We'll get it all figured out and make it official as soon as we can."

"Do to the time it will take to get everything done, you will need to have a new ceremony. The vows you took, since you didn't get the license in advance, won't count. We could let a day or two slide, as was the case for this, but you're looking at a thirty day wait before you can begin the annulment process."

"What the hell did you just say?" Ky snapped. "Why would Bea have to wait thirty days?"

"It's the law in Georgia. A married couple must be separated for thirty days before they can file…"

"We were never married!" I shouted at him.

"Ma'am, I understand. Let's go to my office," He suggested after the people who were waiting for us to finish started to grumble about the wait.

We followed Judge Harrington down the hall and through several doors before we ever made it to his office. Once we were there, he called who I assumed was the security person he spoke to previously and told him to have everyone come to his office instead of the clerk's.

As we waited, my temper started to flare. "I don't understand why I have to wait the legal time for a real married couple when none of this was legal."

"I understand your frustration, ma'am. It's not fair that you're tied up by the letter of the law when Lawson Gregory allegedly had someone forge your signature."

"Not allegedly. He did that. Look," I pointed to the copy of the signed marriage certificate that had been entered into the county records. "That is not anything like my signature."

"I understand." The man blew out a heavy sigh. "My Aunt Bette should have retired a few years ago. Her husband died and her retirement got put on hold indefinitely without his income to help out."

"I feel bad that your aunt was put in that position, but realistically, she should have told them to come back when both people had proper identification."

"You're absolutely right. She should have. I just wanted to explain that she's a romantic at heart and thought she was doing the right thing."

"That's not how official positions work though," Ky stated. I turned to see the angry scowl on his face aimed at the man. "Excuses like that don't fly when the fallout is that I can't be legally married to my best friend. It doesn't fly when you tell the woman who should be MY wife that she has to wait thirty days to do anything about a mixup that wasn't her fault. It was intentional fraud on Law's part and pure ineptitude on the part of the woman who allowed it to happen. I don't care how romantic the notion was, protocols are in place for a reason. This is the reason. My wife, the woman who should be my wife, is now officially married to the man who left her at the altar. Do you understand the ramifications of that?"

"I assure you that I do."

"No, I don't think you do. If we walked out of here today, and ended up in an accident that man is now her next of kin. Legally, your clueless, romantic aunt gave him the right to make life or death decisions over Bea. Those decisions would supersede any her family makes for her. He would inherit from her if she was to die. What if that was his plan all along and your aunt just helped him achieve that goal?"

The judge seemed just as stunned by those revelations as I was. "That can't happen. He can't have that say over me based on a lie."

"We will put some safeguards in place for you while we work through how to handle this situation. I apologize for not having all the answers up front, as this is a unique situation. We will get to the bottom of this and I assure you that I will personally have an injunction against Lawson Gregory having any legal hold on your person or belongings."

"Speaking of belongings," I huffed. "All of my things are still at his condo. We were meant to move in together and get married until he went to chase after another woman. I still need to get my belongings from his house, and after all of this, I'm worried that I will lose everything anyway."

"When we're done here, the sheriff will escort you to his place and stand guard while you obtain all of your possessions. He will also pick up Lawson and bring him in to be booked on fraud charges, so your ex-fiancé won't be there to harass you."

Chapter Thirteen

KY

We got lucky and almost all of Bea's belongings were still packed in their moving boxes. It had been on my mind that the asshole might have unpacked everything to make it more difficult for Bea to move on. It was also convenient that Bea still had a key to the dickwad's place, since he was nowhere to be seen when we rolled up with the sheriff and one of his deputies. They had hoped to make an arrest while assisting us.

Since that didn't happen, the sheriff took off and left the deputy behind just in case Law decided to come back while we were there. Bea's dad, brother, cousin, and uncle all came over to pitch in to get things done quicker.

"Seems like only last week we moved this stuff in here," Beckett mentioned.

"That's because it was last week, you moron!" Flynn called back to him. Beckett's ears and cheeks turned red in embarrassment. I thought he had only been teasing before, but his embarrassment suggested that he meant what he said. Flynn always said that he didn't think his cousin was born with a functioning brain. I shrugged it off and grabbed another box to take down to the truck.

"You think this guy will show up?" The deputy asked. He looked bored and even attempted to stifle a yawn as he waited for an answer from Bea.

"He probably already knew not to come home. The asshole saw us going into the courthouse."

"He did?" Bea turned surprised eyes my way.

"Yep. I thought he was just staking the place out to see if we went through with making things official. I'm guessing we just missed him pulling his shady shit. Sandra wasn't with him in the parking lot, so I'm guessing she played her part and took off immediately."

I had identified Sandra as my ex-hookup before we left the courthouse. I still wasn't sure why she would agree to break the law for a man she didn't know. It wasn't like the two of us had ever had anything serious. Sandra had only ever been a once in a while hook up and she had never been in my personal space at all. No rides in my car. Never at my house. The fact that she showed up there the other day completely baffled me because I didn't think she even knew where I lived. It made me wonder if Law hadn't been pulling strings longer than I thought.

I left Bea there to speak with the deputy while I went to grab another box and grabbed two before I walked out with her brother who also had a larger box.

"I think we need to have ourselves a little stakeout and wait for this motherfucker to show his face. The police might get him for fraud, but we all know he'll only get a little slap on the wrist for that shit." Flynn scowled off in the distance as if he could conjure Law out of thin air. "Never liked that smug prick or his family who think they're better than everyone else."

"Believe me, if he shows up anywhere where the cops can't see, I will be in on that plan."

"The cowardly little shit will probably have a camera on him from here on out." That was a thought to keep in mind. It was one thing to give him the ass whopping he deserved. It was another to stoop to his level and end up in jail for assault because there was no doubt Law would press charges if he had proof that it happened.

ONCE WE WERE DONE PACKING everything Bea had stored at Law's place, we took off for her family's home. The whole way, Bea was quiet as I debated the merits of going against her wishes and having everything moved directly to my place. It seemed ridiculous to have to move it all again since I wanted her to live with me.

"You're awful quiet over there."

"I'm trying to figure out why Law would do this. He's not a stupid man, so he has to know that there will be consequences. What he did was illegal. I don't get it."

"He may be relatively intelligent, but he's also a desperate man. The idiot was dumb enough to throw you away and thought he could keep you if he falsely tied you to him."

"Lucky for me the whole 'you don't know what you have until it's gone' thing didn't apply on my end. I knew what I had and I'm honestly thankful he's gone. Well, mostly gone." She huffed out a frustrated breath and then turned toward me. "I don't know if I ever even thanked you for saving my wedding day. It would have been absolutely humiliating if you hadn't stepped in and done what you did."

"I'd do it again, Bea. I hope like hell there will never be another reason for me to step in and be your second-choice groom, now that you know how I feel about you. I'd marry you again today, tomorrow, and every day until I no longer draw breath."

Bea smiled at me. "Of all the things I know about you, the fact that you're such a romantic never even crossed my mind."

"That's because it's a side reserved only for you, sweetheart."

She ducked her head a bit as if to hide her grin and then brought her eyes up to meet mine again. "I like that."

"Good because I love you."

She gasped and then threw her arms around me. "You have always been the best person in my world."

"Except for that rough patch in high school," I tacked on.

"We're going to forget about that time in our history." She shuddered in my arms and for a minute, I wanted to kick my own ass all over again for being such a dumb fuck when I was a teenager. "Okay, well we shouldn't forget it, because it is a really good reminder of how we need to communicate with one another instead of assuming we know what's on the other person's mind. But we'll chalk it up to teenage bullshit and leave it where it belongs - as a life lesson to learn and move on from."

"How did you get so wise, Sweet Bea?"

"I'm awesome like that," she teased with a playful shrug of her shoulders. "I need to go talk to my family. I know Dad has probably told Mom everything, but it still feels like she should hear the whole thing from me, too."

"Bea, you don't need to make excuses for me. If you need your mom, then you do. Let's go."

I could have sworn I heard her sniffle in response but she looked away before I could see her face. Damn, it hadn't been my intention to make her cry. My woman had to do enough of that with all the bullshit Law put her through.

THE MINUTE we arrived at Bea's family home, her mom ran out of the house to meet us and swept her daughter up in her arms. I left them there like that and followed her father into the house. Flynn was there, as was Bea's younger sister, Mina. "Maybe, I should go out there," Mina looked longingly at the stairs instead of the front of the door and Flynn and I laughed at her. Eventually she sighed and slowly meandered out the front door.

"Don't know what's wrong with that girl, but she is the least girly girl I've seen in recent months. It's like all the sweetness has been sucked right out of her and someone put a mopey, withdrawn, darker version of my daughter in its place."

"Has she mentioned anything that might have happened to make her withdraw?" I asked.

Flynn shook his head. "We're all worried about her, especially since she shut out her best friend too. I wonder what that little bitch did to finally make sister wise up to her bullshit. Whatever it was, it took a chunk out of Mina that I don't think we'll ever get back. I better not find out it was something completely unforgivable. I don't care if it was a girl involved, this family is going to get its justice from people who keep fucking with us."

"I have your back on that."

"Can't believe that motherfucker had the audacity to fake a marriage certificate," Flynn added and his father agreed.

"Let's go out on the back lawn, boys. The women will be in soon and they don't need to hear what we plan to do to that good for nothing piece of shit my oldest girl almost married."

I grinned as Flynn threw his head back and cackled. It was rare that Mr. Robeson lost his cool and threw out curse words, but when he did, it was because he meant every word of what he said.

"What are we going to do with the son of a bitch?" Mr. Robeson asked as the three of us stepped out the door.

"Dad, the police will get to him before we will. I think the more pertinent question is what do we do with Bea's stuff?" Both Robeson men turned to look at me. I smiled at them and shrugged my shoulders. "Leave it on the truck for now. I paid to rent it for a few days just in case."

"Just in case what?" Flynn taunted.

"Just in case I can convince your sister to move in with me despite the fact that making our marriage official got put on hold."

Mr. Robeson clapped me on the back and gave a firm nod of his head. "That's my boy. Knew you'd pull your head out of your ass and go after my girl one day."

I laughed along with Flynn. "Dad isn't pulling punches anymore."

"He's right," I said. "Should have done it the day she came back and told me about how that asshole rescued her. Do you know he didn't even want to stop for her that day?"

"Where did you hear that?"

"The asshole's best friend, Todd, was talking about it one night at the bar I was at. He didn't realize I was there. Apparently, he called dibs on Bea and that was when Law changed his mind about helping her. He hadn't noticed her before that. Todd has been butt hurt ever since. I think he would be even more so if he knew the bullshit lies Law told Bea about him."

"What do you mean?" Flynn asked.

"She told me all about how Todd is a dog and uses and throws away women on the regular."

"Are you kidding me?" Flynn cackled. "That idiot can barely get a woman to talk to him because he has zero finesse with the ladies and she believed Law that Todd was some kind of lothario when he was the real one all along?"

"Yep. Law has been an untrustworthy, disloyal dick for a long time."

"It makes me angrier to hear this. My baby had the wool pulled over her eyes for far too long."

"She's making up for it," I said, not thinking about how that came out.

"You respect my girl and treat her right, Kylan Armstrong or I will bury you in a plot right next to the idiot who didn't deserve her before."

"Yes, sir, Mr. Robeson. You have my word. She will always be my priority."

"Good, now that's settled, let's go get a drink. I pray neither of you has girls. They're a blessing for any man until they reach dating age and then it all goes downhill and the gray hairs start to come in quicker. All I can think about is what me and my friends were like at their ages and I understand why scores of fathers have sat at the table cleaning their shotguns when boys have come to sniff around."

"Come on, Dad. Let's get you the strong stuff before you have an aneurysm."

"Fine, fine, but Kylan?"

"Yes, sir?"

"You call me Mr. Robeson one more time and I might get someone to start digging that hole for me. You may not have officially married my daughter, but for all intents and purposes, you are already my son-in-law. You call me Dad now." I gave him a quick nod as we walked back into the house where the women spoke in low tones about how they hoped Law's dick rotted off. Good times.

LATER IN THE EVENING, I finally took Bea back to my place. She wasn't up to staying there with her family overnight. I wasn't about to let her out of my sight. Plus, it seemed harder to convince her to move in with me if we weren't actually at the apartment I planned to share with her.

"I know it's been an emotional day, and you might not be up to anything heavy, so tell me what you're in the mood to eat."

"You don't have to go out of your way, Ky."

I pushed he curls I was so enamored with back from Bea's face and smiled down at her. "I want to get you fed. Carrying around those big emotions is just as exhausting as running full tilt for hours. You need to get some food in your system before you crash." I leaned in and kissed the tip of her perky little nose and then further down so I could claim her perfectly plump lips. "I'll never get enough of tasting these lips," I murmured against them.

"Maybe food can wait," Bea suggested with a comical waggle of her eyebrows. I chuckled, tipped her chin back, and kissed her once more before I shook my head.

"Food first. Then we have all night to explore other things."

After we ate a light dinner, we retired to my bedroom - what I hoped would be 'our' bedroom soon. "Get comfy, you know where my shirts are, if you need something to sleep in." It was my turn to waggle my brows at her. She took it exactly as I hoped and threw her head back in laughter as I made my way to the bathroom. "I'm going to grab a quick shower because I worked up a sweat moving all your boxes earlier."

Bea turned her head to the side and gave a quick sniff. "Oh! Maybe I should join you in there."

My heart thudded to a stop in my chest and then restarted itself into overdrive. We had never showered together and it was one of my top fantasies, but I honestly worried about embarrassing myself and blowing my load all over Bea and the shower stall if she hopped in with me.

"I don't have to," she tacked on timidly when I didn't respond.

"Bea, get your ass in here with me. I only hesitated

because I needed to formulate a plan not to make a fool of myself with you."

She giggled. "How on earth would you make a fool of yourself in the shower? I already know you can't carry a tune to save your life."

I rolled my eyes. "Woman! If you have to ask, you haven't looked at yourself in the mirror lately."

She glanced down at herself cluelessly. "What's that supposed to mean?"

"You are every man's wet dream come true. I'll be lucky if I don't blow my load looking at you before I can even join you in the shower."

A beautiful rose-hued blush stole across her cheeks and pinked the tips of her ears as she ducked her head shyly on the way past me to the bathroom. I took a deep breath and then followed behind my wife-to-be. It really sucked that we hadn't been able to make things official. That was my ultimate dream come true. I wanted to be able to claim Bea as my own in every way.

She stripped off her shirt and then quickly dropped her shorts to her feet. My angelic woman stood there with her lightly tanned skin on display in just a lace bra and panty set in the palest pink. It should have washed her out, but with her dark curls spilled out around her shoulders, it seemed to highlight all her best features instead. "You are a goddess."

"And you're still fully dressed," she tossed back at me as her hands moved behind her back to unlatch the clasps of her bra. I didn't hesitate to give her the same show I enjoyed and ripped my shirt up over my head. My cargo shorts quickly followed along with my socks and boxers. By the time I had everything off, Bea was also blissfully naked. She stood before me, slightly unsure of herself, and I had no clue why.

"Yup, I was right. You are an absolute goddess. If there was ever a perfect model of the womanly form for an artist, it would be you. Hands down, Bea, it would be you." I reached out to touch her and then pulled my hands back as my eyes gazed back up her toned legs to the slightly curved belly and full, rounded breasts. Her dusky nipples played hide and seek through the strands of her hair as they curled down over her shoulders to offer the tiniest hint of modesty. When my eyes finally trailed back up to meet with hers, she was too busy checking out my body to notice. I stood there and let her soak in her fill of me until her eyes also came up to meet mine.

"You look like a sculpture too, except your cock is long and thick, and…"

"Erect?" I questioned. Damn right it was. My soldier stood at attention in front of his Queen and Bea was worth the respect he offered her.

"Yep, that's. Holy crap, Ky, how are you so big?" Her eyes kept dropping below my waist as I chuckled and then moved to adjust the temperature of the water in the shower.

"Come on, sweetheart. Let's get clean so we can dirty ourselves up again in a better way."

Once we were in the shower under the multiple sprays, Bea closed the distance and reached out to touch me. "Is it okay?"

"You never have to ask to touch me, Bea. My body is yours to do with as you please."

"What if I tied you up and rode you like a prized bull?"

"Don't threaten me with a good time, sweetheart. I'm all

for that. Just know that I will return the favor someday." I winked down at her as she bit into her bottom lip. Swear to God, I heard her whimper out a little moan at the thought of me tying her up. It went straight to the top of my to-do list. I had many years of fantasies under my belt where Bea was concerned and she would eventually learn all the dirty, depraved ways I'd dreamed of taking her. Hell, I'd stroked my cock to the thought of having her naked in a shower so many times, I wasn't sure I could pinpoint a number if asked. Still, none of those fantasies compared to the reality of her as she stood before me and took my cock into her hand.

"I can't even fit my fingers around it," she gasped in surprise.

"Bit thicker than some."

"Yeah, no kidding," she huffed as her hand slid up the silky skin and her fingertips teased over the head of my weeping cock. "I'm having a hard time imagining how this monster will feel inside me."

"So good, Bea. I will make it feel better than anything you've ever experienced. That's a promise."

"I have no doubt about that." She kneeled down in front of me and stuck her tongue out to drag over my tip. I threw my head back and gathered her hair up in my fist as gently as possible. The curls were being pulled straight as the water weighed it down.

"God, baby, your mouth on me feels so good. Like a fucking dream."

She moaned and took the entire head into her mouth in response and then she hollowed her cheeks out and sucked me to the back of her throat. "Fuck, Bea!" I glanced down and watched as her mouth spread obscenely around my cock. There was no way she would be able to take me like that too long without her jaw hurting, but I fucking appreciated the hell out of the effort she put in to please me.

"I didn't want this to be all about me, sweetheart." I tugged a bit on her hair to get her attention.

She swatted my thigh and dipped down on my cock again. I hissed as she rubbed her tongue over the sensitive underside of my cock before she sucked hard once more. "Fucking hell!" I could feel her grin at my response before she pulled back and offered a coy smile.

"Get up here," I demanded in a hoarse voice. "We aren't fucking for the first time in the shower. I meant what I said about getting clean, so we can focus on getting dirty." I picked up her shampoo and signaled for her to turn with her back facing me. She shook her head and stepped closer so that we weren't just toe-to-toe, but closer with one of her feet in the middle of mine and the other on the other side of my right foot.

"Are you going to wash my hair for me?" Bea asked in her sweet voice.

"Yeah, sweetheart. Then I'm going to wash that beautiful body of yours."

"Do I get to return the favor?"

"Nope. Not this time. When I'm done, you're going to hop out and go wait for me to finish up. Then, I'm going to come torture you in the best way possible."

Her only response was to tip her head back so I wouldn't get shampoo in her eyes as I massage it into her scalp and down the slick strands of her hair.

After we were both cleaned up, I finally met Bea in the

bedroom. She stood there, naked as the day she was born, and stared at my bed as if she had never seen it before. I walked up, wrapped my arms around my woman, and pulled her back into my front. "What's going on in this pretty head of yours?"

"Honestly, I just wondered if I should climb on the bed and try to get into a sexy position, but then I thought that would be weird. It's strange navigating the newness of this between us. We've always been comfortable around one another and it feels awkward to do the things we never did before. Does that make sense?"

"It tells me you're overthinking it a bit. You could have plopped onto my bed in any ol' position and I would have loved the sight. I've dreamed of seeing you there so many times that no matter how you position yourself it won't be anything I haven't thought about already."

"Are you serious or are you just saying that to make me feel better?"

"Completely serious, Bea. You are the woman I dreamed about when I closed my eyes at night and the one I wished for in the bright light of day too."

"Ky," She whispered.

"Nah, we don't need to get sappy," I mumbled into the skin of her neck. "We need to get you out of your head and into the mood." I nipped at the tender flesh there between her shoulder and neck and delighted in her giggled response.

Bea spun around to face me and her smile nearly knocked me off my feet. "I dreamed about you too, more than I care to admit considering I was with another man for a couple years."

"He doesn't belong here in this moment."

"No, he doesn't, but that doesn't mean you weren't in many moments you had no business being a part of."

"Bea," It was my turn to whisper her name reverently. "Give me those lips," I demanded.

"Which ones?" My woman sassed back.

"That's it!" I picked her up and tossed her onto the bed like she weighed nothing. Then, I dropped down to my knees and crawled to the end of the bed where I grabbed her ankles and pulled her closer until her bottom damn near hung off the edge. "You lost the chance to make that choice for yourself." I dove in and feasted on her pussy. She couldn't even form words for the first two minutes. When she could, I couldn't help but laugh.

"Who said I didn't make my choice?" As she said that, she tugged my head closer to her pretty pussy and I took full advantage and licked her from ass to clit before I stopped to suck and nibble until she squirmed beautifully beneath me. "Ky, please!" She begged as her fingers weaved their way through the strands of my hair.

"Please, what?" I questioned before I went right back to it and started carving out the words, "I love you, Bea" on her clit with my tongue.

"Please, don't stop doing whatever it is that you're doing," she panted.

I groaned against her pussy as I fisted my own shaft and pinched just at the base to get myself back under control. I had been about two seconds from spilling my seed all over the edge of the bed. Just hearing her beg for me to keep pleasuring her was enough to push me to the brink.

"Love this sweet taste, Bea." I swiped my tongue up her

center again. "Think it's my favorite new flavor. Sweet Bea - never knew how accurate that name was until this moment."

"Oh God! I'm never going to be able to hear that without blushing again," she groaned.

I grinned against her pussy and then went back to work until I had her thighs shaking and her pussy pulsing around my fingers as my tongue worked its magic on her clit.

"Ky! God, Ky, don't stop! Fuck, I'm coming!"

I continued to lick her through the orgasm, and only slowed my pace as she began to come down. "That was music to my ears, sweetheart." I reached out and flipped her boneless body over so that her legs hung off the bed and her ass was angled high on the edge of the bed. Then I crawled forward and teased her opening with the head of my dick before I pushed forward and finally, finally after all those years of dreaming of it, sank all the way into Bea's warm, wet cunt.

"Heaven," I grunted. "Sweet fucking heaven, Bea."

"Yeah," she agreed eagerly. "So full, Ky. You have me so full."

I pulled back so slowly it must have been just as torturous for her as it was for me. "No, no, no," she pleaded. I paused for a minute and then slammed back into her without mercy. "Oh! God, yes!" Bea shouted at me as I repeated the movement and then sped it up until I was pumping in and out of her full tilt without holding anything back. "Yes, yes, yes. Ky, fuuuuck!"

"That's it sweetheart. Take my cock. You like it hard, don't you?"

"So much," she managed to get out between labored breaths. "Yes, don't stop. Right there!" Her voice rose in pitch as I hit her G-spot and continued to angle in such a way as I would thrust right over it as I thrust down into her depths.

"Made for me, Bea. You were…" I grunted as her pussy pulsed around my cock. "Fuck, yeah, baby. Fucking perfect for me." She pulsed again and I realized she was about to shoot off like a rocket.

"Ky!" My name whimpered from her lips felt like a fucking reward. I wanted to pound my fucking chest and swim in the pride I felt at taking her to the point where she couldn't even get a one syllable word, like my nickname, past her lips without a whole lot of effort. "Ky!" She wailed as her inner walls clamped down on me. I had never in my life experienced such an amazing fucking sensation. Her muscles squeezed again and I shot off inside her as my arms gripped around her waist and around her front to cup her breasts as I stroked a few more times while we both gradually came down from our equally explosive releases.

"Perfection, Bea." I kissed the back of her neck, then her shoulder, and leaned up further to snatch her lips with mine as she turned her head to the side to meet me for that kiss. It wasn't until I moved to pull out that we both realized we had forgotten something very important.

"You didn't use a condom?" She asked.

"Shit, Bea. I didn't even think. I've never done that before, I swear."

"I know. It's okay. We got carried away. I didn't even realize until I felt everything spill out."

"Stay just like that. Don't move, I'll be right back." I got up and ran to the bathroom to grab a washcloth. I ran it under warm water and came back to the most beautiful sight I had ever seen. My woman was bent over the bed, on her knees, ass in the air, as my come dripped out of her. "I hope we just got you pregnant," I whispered.

"What?" She called out to me and pulled me from the trance I had fallen into from seeing her like that.

"Nothing, sweetheart. Let's get you cleaned up, okay?" I took a minute to gently clean between her legs and then leaned in to drop a kiss on her ass cheek. "Be right back," I whispered as I stood again and went to the bathroom to clean myself off and dispose of the rag.

When I got back out to the bedroom, Bea had hidden herself away under the sheets. She smiled sweetly at me as I climbed into bed beside her. "I kind of hope so too, but then again, I'd really like a couple years of just the two of us together first."

"Sweet Bea," I kissed her lips before either of us could take back our secret wish.

Chapter Fourteen

BEA

I woke up in Ky's arms, and for the first time in as long as I could remember, I felt whole. There is a certain kind of peace to be found when you know you can count on someone to be there for you. I didn't have to worry about what he wanted because Ky had been straight with me the day before. It didn't matter if it took thirty days or thirty years for me to get free of the mess Law created, Ky would be there waiting to marry me the minute I got myself untangled from Law's lies.

I slid a little closer to my man and thought about the night before. We had sex. It was the first time but it felt as though we knew one another intimately all along. There were no fumbling awkward moments of discovery like there had been with the other two men I'd slept with. We were in sync with every touch, kiss, and thrust of our bodies. Sex had never been so all-consuming for me before. It hadn't been terrible with my previous two lovers, but it had definitely been missing something.

"You're thinking awfully hard over there." Ky's sleepy voice rumbled against my neck.

"Nope. I was appreciating how tranquil I felt waking up with you."

I could feel the smile on his lips as he pressed them to my skin and inhaled deeply. "Couldn't have said it better myself," he mumbled. "Thought I was dreaming again."

"You've had dreams of waking up spooned with me?"

"Sweet Bea, I've had dreams of waking up wrapped around your body, going to sleep next to you at night, fucking you all night long, and things as mundane as eating a meal with you knowing that you're mine. You have always been the dream."

My response was nothing more than a whimper because it took me a moment to process exactly what he'd said. I was his dream. Every aspect of being with me had been featured. A tear slipped free of my eyes and Ky turned me over so that I rolled beneath him. His eyes took me in as his body hovered above me. The warmth of him radiating down to me, as if he shared his very life force with me. "I meant every word, Bea. This is a dream come true and won't ever let go without a fight."

"That's good because it is a dream come true for me too. I convinced myself a long time ago that it would only ever be a dream, so I'm having a hard time processing just how real this is."

He leaned in and crashed his lips down on mine. Ky licked at the seam of my lips and they immediately parted to allow him in. There were no thoughts of morning breath or regrets for what might happen to our friendship. We were both adults now. We knew our own minds, and more importantly, we knew one another's hearts too.

Ky nipped at my bottom lip as he pulled away. "I know we dropped everything off at your family's house yesterday, but I'd really love it if you brought it all here. We don't need to be officially married to start our lives together."

"Are you serious? You don't want to take some time to see how this goes first?" I hoped like hell he said no, but the insecurities that had grown in the aftermath of Law's betrayal made me hesitate enough to ask.

"Bea, it's not like we're strangers dating for the first time. We've been best friends practically our whole lives. We know just about everything there is to know about one another. It's not a far stretch to move in even though we just entered into a romantic relationship less than a week ago."

"Oh God!" I threw my hands over my face. "It hasn't even been a week. What must people think of us?"

"Does it really matter? I love you. I have always loved you. We just finally realized the feeling might be mutual and besides, we have a stronger foundation to build on than most couples just starting out. We've been friends for a lifetime."

"Yeah, I know. I guess I'm a little thrown by what happened with Law. Not just this latest stunt of his, but all of it. Will you want to leave me too, once we live together and you realize that I drool so much I have to turn my pillow over in the middle of the night to avoid the puddle I created?"

Ky laughed at me. "Sweet Bea," he whispered against my cheek. "I already know all about your drooling habits."

"What? How?"

"It's not like you've never fallen asleep on me during one

of our movie nights. Pretty obvious when you leave a puddle behind on my shirt."

"Damn, and I thought I had you fooled all this time." I teased even though part of me was mortified. Granted, it wasn't like Ky would hold anything against me, even the things I could help, but definitely not the things that were out of my control.

"Come on, I thought we got past all the embarrassing stuff a long time ago. Remember the first time I farted in front of you and nearly shit my pants?"

I threw my head back and laughed with my whole body as the memory came back to me. "Oh my God!" I huffed out between giggles. "You ran so fast with your knees locked to get to the house. To this day, I have never seen anything like it."

"I'm willing to bet money that your mom has a little bit of PTSD. Every time I come into the house too quickly, she jumps and makes way for me to get by like I might shit on her feet."

His admission made me laugh even harder. I swiped at a tear that fell from my eyes. "Oh, Ky, I can't believe I forgot about that. Mom even side-eyed me for a couple weeks after that. She kept checking to make sure I didn't have an upset stomach for fear that I might repeat your performance. I'm pretty sure you were the reason she had the downstairs bathroom remodeled that year."

Ky's whole body shook as he laughed. "If I can talk about that and laugh with you over my shitty past, I think you're safe to drool around me."

"Fair enough. I guess that's settled then."

"What is settled? I had the most embarrassing moment between us so far?"

I shook my head. "Well, that too, but it's settled that I'll move in now." I bit into my lower lip and glanced up at him through my lashes. "If you are really sure about it."

"Never been surer of anything in my life, beautiful."

"We should have just brought all my stuff here earlier. Now, we'll have to move it all again."

Ky shook his head. "The truck was never unloaded. All your things are ready to come here in the morning."

"In the morning, huh?"

"Yup." He leaned in and placed a kiss on my nose. "We might be too worn out to do it first thing in the morning, but we'll get to it eventually."

"I'll run out of things to wear," I insisted.

"Don't threaten me with a good time," He teased.

"Then stop withholding my good time, Kylan Armstrong."

"Your wish is my command, Beatrice Armstrong."

I scrunched my nose up at the use of my full first name. "You did not just full name me instead of getting me naked."

"You full-named me first." He leaned down and brushed his lips against mine before the biggest grin I'd ever seen on my best friend broke out across his face. "I like that you accepted my name as yours now, whether it is legal or not."

Heat bloomed in my cheeks as a shroud of embarrassment engulfed me. "I practiced it a lot when we were younger."

"Oh? Did you practice signing your married name?"

"Shut up and get me naked, Kylan."

"As you wish, Beatr-"

I smacked him in the gut - which was actually well-toned muscle - and he let out a playful "Oof". "You know better."

"Fine, Sweet Bea. Let's get naked and fuck."

I giggled more about his teasing tone than anything else because that sounded like the best way to relax into what was left of another mostly crappy day. Ky's soulful eyes found mine and my giggles faded as the passion between us ignited.

"Are you sore from before?" He asked cautiously.

I shook my head. "Maybe a little, but in a good way. It's more like," I ducked my head, embarrassed to admit the next part.

"More like?" Ky encouraged.

"More like I know you were there. There's no pain, just..." I huffed. "It's hard to explain."

"No need, sweetheart. I wanted to make sure you were okay if we went there again so soon. I know you weren't a virgin, but I'm probably a good bit thicker than the men you were with."

"That's a bit of an understatement," I agreed. I could almost see his chest swell with pride. "Oh my God, you are such a man. You all love to compare dick sizes, don't you?"

He shrugged and smirked at me. "It is a bit of an ego boost when you always come out on top. I was blessed with size and the ability to pay attention to what my woman needs. I'd say you should thank God for that, but you already did."

I playfully swatted at his chest. "You are ridiculous."

"I'm honest, sweetheart. There's nothing wrong with being honest, is there?"

"Only when you forget to be humble." I leaned in and kissed the underside of his chin. "Then again, I suppose you don't really need to be humble with me where your bedroom progress is concerned."

"Bedroom prowess, huh?" He chuckled and rolled me to my back. "How about I show you a different kind of bedroom moves?"

"What kind would those be?"

"The kind where I make love to the woman who will be only mine until the end of our days."

"Ky, my heart squeezes so tight every time you say something like that. I'm afraid one day you'll take my breath away completely."

"Then I'll just have to breathe life back into you, Sweet Bea. You're it for me, and there is no way in hell I'm ever letting you go now that I've had you in my arms the way I always dreamed."

Ky reached between us and slid his fingers along my already slick center. "Thank fuck," he hissed as he lined himself up and then slowly pushed in until he was fully seated inside me. I felt filled to the brim with him, as if there wasn't another millimeter of space.

"It's like you were made to fit perfectly inside me," I whispered into his shoulder as he brought his body down to lie as close to mine as possible. My nipples perked up with each of his thrusts as they dragged through the crisp hairs on his chest. Ky's pubic bone slid across my clit with each roll of his hips as our bodies moved together and his hands roamed from my shoulders to my chest and down between our bodies to tease and torment my clit as he plucked and pulled on it while never losing the rhythm of his thrust.

When his mouth crashed down on mine, it was almost a sensitivity overload. I whimpered into his mouth as he groaned above me and nipped at my lip.

I was made for you, sweet girl. The same way you were made for me. Love how your body lines up just right. You feel that, Bea? So many sensations all at once and I can see from that faraway expression that you're damn near over-loading already. We're nowhere near close to being done though, so I'm going to back off a bit for now."

"No," I managed to choke out.

"Oh yeah, I think my beautiful girl needs to learn a lesson in delayed gratification."

"I think all the years we spent without one another like this was delayed enough, don't you?"

"Fuck," he mumbled into my shoulder. "How can I argue with that?"

Even though he agreed with me, Ky still pulled his body up so that he balanced himself above me on his hands with his arms out straight at my sides. He continued the slow and steady hip roll that had the head of his penis drag over over my g-spot and then his pubic bone slid across my clit. My nerves were still wrapped tight and felt like they were on a fragile precipice that could give way at any moment.

"You're so beautiful." He reached up and tucked my still damp locks down beside my shoulder. "Dreamed of this hair draped across my pillow."

"Dreamed of you looking down at me like that," I admitted. The smile that bloomed on his face nearly took my breath away, like he threatened to do earlier. "You are so damn handsome, Ky."

"Oh Bea," he growled as he picked up the pace and

thrust harder into my body. I rocked my hips up to meet his body with my own and joyed in the needy grunt he released. I pushed my hand up through his silky hair that had fallen over and covered his eye. Then I closed my fist around the hair and held on tight as he lifted my waist and pulled me into him even harder. Ky was mostly on his knees at that point while his hands wrapped around my hips and he pushed me away and pulled me back to him like I was his little fuck doll.

"I'm going to pump so much come into you that you won't have a choice but to get pregnant."

I wished that were true. It was the entirely wrong time of the month for his wish to be granted. I figured that out after our first round of unprotected sex. I hadn't wanted to broach the subject then, and it wasn't really conducive to do so with him inside me either, but I'd never had sex without a condom before him. I'd never had such powerful, fulfilling sex either.

"You with me, Sweet Bea?"

"I'll always be with you."

Chapter Fifteen

KY

Two DAYS after we got Bea's things settled into our place, my phone rang with an unknown number. Normally, I'd just ignore those calls, but something made me pick that one up.

"Thank fuck!" I heard an all-too familiar voice grumble as the line connected.

"Who is this?" I asked the question even though I already knew the answer because he didn't deserve to know that anyone in Bea's life would recognize him.

"It's Law."

I laughed in response and almost hung up until I heard him groan. "I know I did a shitty thing. Wasn't thinking. She won't take my calls."

"She has you blocked, and for good reason, asshole."

"I know," he moaned again, like I would have any sympathy for him. "I wanted to make things right. I will sign annulment papers or whatever she wants me to do, if she'll drop the criminal charges." My laughter should have sufficed as his answer. "What the hell, Kylan? I'm being serious and trying to fix the situation."

"The situation you created by committing fraud?"

"I wasn't thinking."

"You were thinking clearly enough to get an accomplice to help you."

"Yeah, and don't you give a single damn about your ex-girlfriend? She's facing charges too, and all because she's in love with you."

"She's not in love with me. She can't possibly be because she loves herself too much to care about anyone else. Plus, Sandra was never a girlfriend to begin with. I honestly don't give two fucks what happens to her. She chose to play that game with you and now she has to live with the consequences." He stayed silent on the other end, so I let him know that his efforts were wasted. "You do too. Bea can't ask them to drop the charges because you were caught on camera, in the courthouse, committing fraud. They literally have video of what you did and of Bea and me coming in to make things official, only to learn that thanks to you and a technicality, she's already married. Not legally, mind you, but you've caused us enough headaches, you couldn't possibly think either of us would do you a favor even if it was within our power."

"You're an asshole, Ky."

"No, Law, you're the asshole for leaving a good woman at the altar, for faking a marriage on paper with her, and prolonging her misery because she's unwillingly attached to you."

"She said yes to marrying me." He yelled down the line.

"Yep, and then she said 'No' to you when you left her a note saying you were interested in another woman."

"I did the right thing!" He yelled.

"No, you didn't. The right thing would have been for you to call things off when you first realized you didn't love Bea enough to not get carried away with another woman. This is really a pointless conversation though. We're only a couple weeks from having your mess fixed and then Bea is all mine. Thanks, by the way. I appreciate you fucking up so I could get my woman back in my arms. I stupidly let her go because I thought SHE would be happier before. I won't make that mistake again."

"You really don't care that they'll put me in jail, do you?" Once again, my laughter was the only response that seemed to fit his question. "Well, I bet Bea cares." The asshole insisted rather smugly.

I glanced over to the bed, where Bea still slept. "You really think so? After what you put her through?" He didn't answer but I could hear his huff of indignation down the line. "Her wild, dark curls are spilled out all over my pillow and hers right now. She's on her side facing the part of the bed I only just vacated a few minutes before your call. Her arm is stretched out like she's trying to find me there. She looks so peaceful and serene in her sleep, even with the drool she's collected on the pillow beneath her." I chuckled a bit at that because it was true. While they hadn't lived together before, they had spent nights with one another, so I knew the fucker could picture exactly what I was talking about. "She spent last night with her arms and legs wrapped so tight around me that I didn't think I'd ever get free. Not that I wanted to. If I didn't have to go to work today, I'd still be there snuggled up to the best woman in the world. You remember her - the woman you threw away for a missed opportunity with someone else." I chuckled again as I heard his breathing increase right alongside his growing anger. "You had the perfect woman and now you'll go to jail for trying to claim her when she wasn't yours to claim anymore. Both of those things are one hundred percent your fault and I thank you for them."

I hung up and glanced back up to see that Bea was awake. "That was some speech. I'm assuming Law called you for some reason?"

"He said he would sign annulment papers or whatever was necessary if you would withdraw the criminal charges."

My beautiful woman laughed. "I don't have any control over those criminal charges. He did what he did in full sight of the security cameras and witnesses, including the woman whose job is on the line as a result."

"Told him that too, but you were still asleep for that part."

"So, you think I'm the perfect woman, huh?"

"Drool and all, baby!"

She threw her swampy pillow at me, and as luck would have it, the wet spot is what caught me in the face. That wasn't something I'd ever complain about.

"Do you have to go to work today?"

I nodded. "Took as much time off as I'm able to right now. Some of us don't get summers off like you, lucky girl."

"I'm thinking about looking for a part time job this summer. I need something to keep me busy. She seemed worried about how I would react, so I moved to her side and smiled down at her.

"Bea, you do whatever is best for you. You want a summer job to keep you occupied, get one. If you don't want one and want to work on hobbies or just laze around the house all day, that's fine too. Whatever makes you happy."

"You mean that, don't you?"

"Of course, I do. Why wouldn't I want you happy?"

"It's like night and day. I don't know how I stayed with Law as long as I did. Every time you prove what his answers should have been, it makes me wonder why I didn't put it all together before now." She huffed and blew a curl out of her face as she sat up with her back to the headboard.

"What do you mean?"

"When I told Law that I wanted to get a little side job for the summer, he almost lost his mind. Of course, I'd done it in front of his mother during Sunday brunch, and she had the same opinion as her son. They had the nerve to tell me that my time off should be about being there for Law and whatever he needed. Another job would mean time sacrificed. It's not like he wouldn't still be working." She huffed again. "His mother suggested that I hand deliver Law's lunch to him every day and he was in complete agreement with her."

"That whole family has issues."

"I can't believe I almost married into that mess. What was I thinking?"

"It doesn't matter now. We have one another, and I'm all for whatever schedule will make you happy." If I knew how to make that smile on Bea's face permanent, I would bottle the sentiment and make sure to give her healthy doses of it on the regular. Unfortunately, the alarm on my cell phone rang out and I realized that I would be late if I lingered any longer.

"Sorry, Sweet Bea, I have to get to work. There's

nothing more I want right now than to lay you flat on this bed and eat you up from bottom to top, but I am out of time. So, stew on that all day while you think about where you want to work. Tonight, we'll make it happen." I winked at her and watched as she ducked her head and blushed. Fuck, but that was a sight. The woman was too mature to blush the way younger women did. Then again, she had two lovers in her life, and I doubted either of them were that good, so it was kind of like she was still all fresh and new. I cherished every fucking blush she gave me and hoped to see more.

"Bea," I called just as I got to the bedroom door.

"Yeah?"

"I love you."

"I love you, too, Ky." The words were almost a whisper and I could see the shine of tears in her eyes as she spoke. There was a part of her that Law had damaged. That asshole made her believe she wasn't worthy, but it was now my life's mission to disabuse her of that silly notion. My woman was perfect and damn if I'd allow her to behave as though she had reason to doubt that.

Chapter Sixteen

BEA

AFTER KY LEFT FOR WORK, I didn't know what to do with myself. He told me to make myself at home, as it was my place now too, but that still felt strange. It felt as though I was an uninvited guest in my best friend's home. Yes, it was dumb to feel that way because I knew Ky did not see it that way at all. Still, I couldn't help that nagging voice of anxiety in the back of my mind that filled me with self-doubt after being ditched by my original fiancé during my wedding.

Damn Law. If he only knew the damage he had done. Not that he would care. As I had started to realize far too late, Law only cared about himself and how things affected him.

I decided to put all my newfound insecurities aside and go out into town to look for a job that would keep me occupied for the rest of the summer. Getting showered was a strange experience where I ended up sniffing Ky's body wash for far too long. It smelled like him, and his scent had always brought me comfort. He would probably tease me relentlessly if he knew. I thought that right up until I noticed that my own body wash had been moved from where I'd put it the night before. Maybe Ky wouldn't tease me after all.

Once I was ready, had my curls tamed, and grabbed all my important documents I left to go search a few places close to Ky's place. Our place. It was weird to think about living with him now. While we may have already known one another more than two people who just started dating, there was still a strangeness to how quickly we went from best friends to almost married and living together.

I almost passed by a daycare that was only a block over from where I now lived, but children's laughter caught my attention. Two frazzled looking women attempted to round up a class of toddlers from their fenced-in playground, but the kids played a good game of distraction and dodge. Some would run away from their teachers again the minute another one would offer up a good enough distraction.

Toddlers were diabolical, but also hilarious. I giggled the whole way into the building where I introduced myself to the owner of the facility.

"Hi, can I help you?"

"I hoped to speak to someone in charge of hiring or whoever runs this place."

"Why? Did you have an issue with one of our employees?" The lady, who appeared to be about my mother's age, asked as she gave me a bit of side eye.

"No, I happened to be passing by on my way to go look for summer employment. I'm a language arts teacher at the middle school over on Jackson St. I will go crazy without something to do this summer, and I thought you might need the help."

The woman, Suzanne Richards, looked up toward the

ceiling and mumbled something about answered prayers. "We need to run a background check and get all your information, including a tuberculosis test, but if you could start next week and your background and a call to the school board checks out, we would love to have you. We always lose employees temporarily for the summer. I guess the women who have children and don't want to pay the daycare fee so that they can work in a daycare, decide that we don't need the help in the summer."

"That's awful. I'm happy to step in and fill someone's shoes for the summer, though."

"Come back to my office and I'll get the paperwork for you to fill out. I don't suppose you have your birth certificate and social security card on you?"

"I do. I figured I should come prepared in case I got lucky."

"Please, tell me you haven't filled out applications for a better job."

I shook my head and smiled at Suzanne. "Nope. This was the first place I stopped when the children's laughter outside caught my attention."

She grinned knowingly. "Ah, you caught them playing bait and switch games with their teachers, hmm?"

"I did. I love that age. They're always a delightful challenge."

"I'm happy to hear you think so because they're probably the group I'll put you with. Marissa normally works with the infants, but she had to fill in when one of our girls decided to take unofficial 'summer leave'." Suzanne rolled her eyes as she said the last bit.

"That must be frustrating."

"It is, but it also isn't your concern, so that's the last I'll say about it beyond thanking you for wanting to fill in for people who can't be here during the months you're off work for the public schools." She riffled through a file cabinet and then produced a stack of papers with an "Ah-ha!".

"You can fill these out at home, if you like, or you could do it here and save some time coming back."

"Thank you," I said after taking the stack of papers. I pulled a pen out of the cup that held several on Suzanne's desk and started to fill out the forms.

"Can I ask why you work with middle school children if you enjoy the toddler age so much?"

I continued to fill out the form as I answered her. "I also love middle school kids."

Suzanne giggled. "I think you're the first teacher I've ever heard say that and sound as though they meant it."

"Oh, I do mean it. They're on the cusp between child-hood and the teen years. It's one of the biggest discovery times in adolescence. Sure, they get super hormonal and my goodness do they stink some days." Suzanne giggled along with me at that revelation. "They're also so eager to learn and their curiosity hasn't been sapped quite yet. I've worked with high school students and even elementary ages, but middle school is the sweet spot in between. They still have a bit of innocence. I don't know. It's kind of magical. I guess I love them for the same reason toddlers grab my attention. They're in the transition between being babies and big kids. I guess I like the in between ages."

"Well, it sounds like you'll be a perfect fit here." After I handed Suzanne all of my paperwork and stood to shake her hand, she passed along a list of things I needed to get done before she could put me on the schedule. Besides fingerprinting for the background check, I had to get the TB test, and couldn't start until the results for both of those came back.

"Well, now I have to figure out what to do with the rest of my day." I laughed. "I honestly anticipated my job search would take me a lot longer today."

"I am glad you decided to start here. You just took a little weight off my shoulders."

"Happy to help. I'll get these taken care of today and bring the results for the TB test back as soon as I can get it done."

"It only takes a few days," Suzanne reassured me. "The background check information will come straight to me from the Sheriff's Department."

Since I didn't have to waste time looking for employment, I went to the health department to get my TB test, then went to the Sheriff's office to get my fingerprints done for my background check. It always amused me that it would be blank, since I'd never even had a speeding ticket, let alone committed a crime, but I understood the need to check.

After all that was done, it was almost lunchtime, so I decided to check to see when Ky would be taking lunch.

Bea: Hey, already did all the things to be hired for my new job. When are you going to lunch? Maybe we can have a quick celebration.

Ky: Can't today. I'm putting out some fires that started to smolder while I was off work.

Bea: Okay, let me know if you need me to bring you something. I don't mind.

Ky: No need. See you tonight for dinner. Love ya.

Bea: Love you too.

The sigh that left my body was pure disappointment. This was exactly why I needed a job to keep me busy during the summer months. I didn't do good in my own company. I had just rounded the corner and was only a few steps away from the entrance to Ky's - our - condo when the screech of someone's brakes and then the squeal of tires locking up made me snap my head around just in time to see a car coming for me. I jumped back and plastered myself to the building beside Ky's and just barely missed being hit by the ugliest rust and green Cadillac I had ever seen.

The car missed me by only a couple inches. When I finally got a look at the driver, I was stunned. "Are you kidding me?" I yelled. A couple people had come out of the coffee shop across the street to see what in the world was going on.

"You ruined my life!" Sandra screeched at me. "Ky was supposed to be mine!"

"Oh my God! Are you serious? You just tried to hit me with your car because your hookup didn't want to date you?"

"He was more than a hookup!" Her pitchy voice yelled. I should have known better than to taunt her because Sandra's vehicular homicide attempt was the end of her plan. It had been a warm up because opportunity struck before she could get up to Ky's apartment to get to me. "He's the love of my life."

"You're nuts!" I shouted at her, which was the wrong thing to do because she jumped from her car and started to run for me. I wasn't that far away and she had a knife in her hand. A freaking knife. And it wasn't a tiny little steak knife either. It looked like something a serial killer from a horror movie would wander around with so they could chop up unsuspecting strangers.

"You really are nuts!" I yelled. Again, probably not the best way to deescalate the situation, but my brain was a little slow to process the fact that someone wanted to kill me. I vaguely heard someone yell that they called 9-1-1, but they wouldn't get here fast enough.

"You think you're better than me?"

"Lady, I don't even know you!"

"You stole my man and then I pretended to be you so that pathetic man you were meant to marry could be legally married to you. You were supposed to go back to him after that."

"I was…?" Yeah, I had no words for that. Sandra had lost her ever-loving mind somewhere along the way. She didn't bother to hear me out, or to see reason, and instead jumped forward as she brought her knife wielding arm down in a stabbing motion I was not the least bit comfortable with. I had a building at my back, a dumpster to my left, and her coming at me from the front. I tried to throw myself to the left - toward the sidewalk and road - but didn't manage in time.

The knife cut through my arm like heated steel through butter. I screamed as momentum took me down to my knees and then gasped out a few obscenities as my knees and hip hit the ground just before I rolled right onto the arm that had been slashed by Ky's crazy ex-hookup.

Sandra threw her head back and gave a banshee-like shriek before coming for me again. I had nowhere to go because it was hard to scamper up off the ground with a busted knee, bruised hip, and slashed up arm. Luckily for me, a do-gooder ran over and tackled Sandra before she could stick me with her murder stick again.

"You crazy bitch!" I yelled as the man who tackled Sandra flipped her over so she was lying on the ground on her stomach. He sat on her and held her knife wielding hand down until his buddy could pry the damn thing out of her fingers.

A woman ran over once Sandra was secured, and kneeled down beside me. "I called 9-1-1. They're sending an ambulance." She looked at my wounded arm and clucked out a weird noise. "She did a number on your arm." She then tried to yell into the crowd. "Does anyone have any bandages? We need to get this bleeding stopped."

"Here!" A teenage boy ran out of the coffee shop carrying a small first aid kit.

"Not sure anything in there will suffice for this," the woman lamented. "Let's have a look anyway."

Before the stranger could try to play doctor with me, we all heard the wailing sirens of the ambulance and police cars that responded to the emergency call. "Thank God!" I mumbled as a shiver ran through me.

"I've never seen anything like that before," the boy from he coffee shop admitted.

"Welcome to the club," I muttered as I tried to shift into

a more comfortable position. My arm screamed at me as did my knee, so I stopped moving and decided uncomfortable was better than added pain.

"Did you really steal her man?" The boy asked tactlessly.

"No. Ky is my best friend and that woman is nuts. She pretended to be me and signed a marriage certificate with my ex-fiancé - not Ky - so the police were looking for her for the fraud case."

"Wow, you live an exciting life."

"I really wish I didn't."

Two police officers and a couple EMTs came over to assess the situation. I felt nauseous by then and listened as the bystanders relayed what happened. Sandra stopped all her shrieking and wailing as she was handcuffed. The knife was collected into an evidence bag, and someone told the police they got everything on video, including the attempt to hit me with the car.

The EMTs bandaged up my arm and then pulled a gurney up beside me. "Pretty sure I can walk," I croaked out.

"Ma'am, I just gave you something for the pain that will make you unsteady on your feet and we don't know the extent of the damage that was done. It is safer for us to get you on the board and up onto the gurney for transport."

"Okay." My one-word response was nothing more than a whisper. My day had started so promising and quickly turned to absolute shit. "My purse?" I questioned.

"Got it," the other man stated. "I'll make sure it comes with you."

"Thank you."

My eyes drooped and my arm felt like a throbbing noodle attached to me instead of the painful, bloody catastrophe of moments ago.

"Get some rest. By the time you wake up, you'll be at the hospital for some stitches in that arm."

WHEN I WOKE up it was to a doctor smiling at me as he put the last stitch into my arm. "Holy crap, what did that man give me, a horse tranquilizer?"

The doctor chuckled. "Nothing that potent, though it seems you probably didn't need as big a dose as he gave you." He smiled as he took in my hair. "Probably thought all those beautiful curls weighed more than they do."

"No flirting with my wife, Doc." I glanced over to my right to see Ky stood there. His hair was in disarray as if he had been tugging at it. His eyes tracked every movement the doctor made as if he thought he could do better.

"Ky, when? How did you get here?"

"The usual way. One of my neighbors, Josh Manus, is the man that tackled Sandra. As soon as the cops had her cuffed, he called me to let me know what happened. I drove straight here."

"How did he know to call you? I only moved in yesterday."

"Sweet Bea," His eyes took on a softer look. "Every man in my building has been asking about you since I moved in. They've seen you coming and going from my place. Josh was one who hoped you were my sister." He chuckled at that and the doctor joined him and nodded his head as if he had a similar thought. My cheeks heated with what I was sure would be a visible blush.

"How long have you been here?"

"I got here the same time the ambulance pulled up outside. Been by your side the whole time."

A relieved sigh left me. "Thank you." I turned to the doctor, "No offense," I said before looking back toward Ky, "it scared me to think of what might have happened to me with me being so out of it. Whatever that EMT gave me hit me hard and fast."

"He was a paramedic, and we've already addressed the issue with him."

"Thank you. What happened to Sandra?" I asked as I turned back to Ky. "Did they lock her up? Is she still there? I hope they didn't let her back out." Panic started to take over as I thought about the fact that the crazy woman knew where I lived.

"Maybe we should wait a bit to talk about that situation, Ms. Robeson. We don't need your heart rate going crazy."

"Sorry, but what if she comes after me again?"

Ky stepped forward and made his way to my other side. "You don't have to worry about her. She's been charged with a felony in the fraud case, attempted vehicular homicide, and attempted murder as a second incident since the car didn't hit you. She's also facing an assault with a deadly weapon charge. Your dad and Flynn are down at the courthouse talking to the magistrate in the hopes that he can put in a word about keeping her until trial for your safety."

I rolled my eyes. "They do realize everyone gets due process, right? They can't just demand that she not be released."

Ky shrugged. "If I didn't need to be here by your side, I would be there doing the same damn thing, Bea."

"Well," I didn't know what to say to that. "I'm glad you're here."

"I have it on good authority that even if the judge sets bail, it will be high, and she won't be able to pay."

"All done here," The doctor broke into our conversation to say. "We'll get you down to radiology shortly to check out your knee and hip to make sure there were no fractures. I think they're both just bruised and sore. The knee swelled quite a bit, but we gave you something for the swelling and iced it down while you were out."

I glanced down as he started to wrap a bandage around my arm. "How many stitches is that?" My arm was stitched from the middle of my bicep in an arcing line to the outside of my mid forearm. It seemed to hurt again the minute I looked at it.

"There are 44 stitches. You'll need to come back and have them removed in about seven days."

"That sounds like a load of fun." I rolled my eyes to indicate the level of sarcasm that went with my statement.

"It won't be as bad as getting them put in."

"Considering I was unconscious for most of that, I think you might be lying to me, Doc."

He grinned and patted my leg. A low growl came from my other side and I turned to see Ky staring daggers at the man's hand. The doctor snatched his hand back and laughed nervously. "Right. Well, we'll see you in seven days to get those stitches out and a nurse will come by shortly to wheel you down to radiology for those X-rays. Once we get a look at them and make sure there are no fractures, we'll get you discharged with care instructions for the wound. I hope the person who did this to you is kept behind bars so it doesn't happen again."

"That makes two of us," I mumbled as he left. Then my eyes landed on Ky's. "Did you really just growl at my doctor?"

"He shouldn't have touched you."

"He just patted my leg reassuringly."

"Well, I was about to reassure him that you were taken. You were playing sleeping beauty too long and missed the way he appreciated the view."

"Ew, that's creepy."

Ky shook his head. "You're a beautiful woman, Bea. Even when you're drooling on yourself and mumbling nonsense about your husband's exes." He grinned at the last bit.

"No, I didn't."

"Oh, you did. It was cute. I think you were plotting your revenge on Sandra while you were knocked out."

"Well, that's a shame because I don't remember what I came up with and now I have to start from scratch."

"I was so damn scared, Bea."

"You and me both. She tried to run me over and then stabbed me. If I hadn't tried to tuck and roll she would have gotten me in the chest."

"I'm so fucking sorry. I swear to you, she never seemed crazy and we were never serious enough for her to even be that bonkers about me."

"Stop." I whispered as he took the hand on my unin-jured side into his own. "You don't have to explain anything to me. Did you forget we were best friends this whole time? I knew about your hookups with Sandra, that they were few and far between, and that she was never even worthy of a mention by you to me. Any girl you have ever been close to serious about - enough to date them semi-regularly - you have told me about. I only knew about Sandra in passing because Law told me he saw you with her."

"I've been wondering about that, actually." Ky seemed to be looking over my shoulder, but he was lost in thought for a moment before his attention returned back to me. "It's weird that Sandra was ever on the scene. We didn't cross paths normally and then suddenly, six months or so ago, she was everywhere I was. She knew where I lived even though I never brought her home with me. The way she showed up to my home out of the blue when Law was there and then conveniently showed up to the courthouse with Law..." He shook his head as if the thought was too preposterous.

"You think Law set her on you to begin with?"

Ky nodded his head. "I'm not sure why, but yeah, it feels that way considering everything that has happened."

"Why would he do that?"

"Maybe he thought Sandra would keep my mind off my feelings for you." Ky stared at me a moment before his cocky grin appeared. "You might have been oblivious about my feelings for you, but Law never was. That's why he pushed so hard for you to ditch our friendship."

"If I find out he set this bullshit into motion-" I was cut off before I could say more as a nurse came into the room with Law hot on her heels.

"Ms. Robeson, you already have your husband back here with you, but this man just proved to us - with a copy of your marriage certificate - that he is indeed your *real* husband." Two security guards stood at the door ready to pull Ky from the room.

"That man is wanted by the police. He is part of the reason I am in here. The woman who signed that marriage certificate, while pretending to be me, is the one who attacked me today."

"Jesus, I am so sorry, Bea. I can't believe Sandra would do this to you."

I glanced at Ky, seeing that he also noted the familiarity with which Law spoke of Sandra. "Did you know Sandra this whole time?" I asked.

Law's face flushed and then drained of color in an instant. "I didn't think… I never meant for any of this to happen. She was supposed to distract Ky. I swear, that was all. When I started paying more attention to Jackie, I knew you would lean on Ky. I wanted him out of the picture while I made my mind up about who I wanted most."

I scrunched my nose in disgust. "Please, call the police and don't let this man escape. He is partially responsible for the attack on me today."

"No! I'm not. That's what I came to tell you. Sandra called me from jail and wanted me to bail her out. At first I thought it was just the fraud thing with having her sign the marriage certificate in your name. When she told me why, I hung up on her and came directly here."

"You really shouldn't have." I turned toward the guards who nodded at me. I guessed that meant they alerted the police. I squeezed Ky's hand tighter because it felt as though he would get up and go after Law at any moment and the last thing I needed was for him to get into trouble as a result of my ex's crap.

Chapter Seventeen

KY

I COULDN'T BELIEVE the stones on Bea's ex-fiancé. The fact that Law showed up with that bogus marriage certificate pissed me off to the point of seeing red. If it weren't for the death grip Bea had on my hand, I would have already put a fist through his fucking teeth.

"You need to get that motherfucker muzzled before he says anything else." I warned the guards.

"If it helps, we have everything he said on body cam, since we were recently equipped with them for the times when we have to remove someone from the premises."

Ky nodded and I felt him relax a bit. "That's good. Then the prosecutor will be interested to hear that Lawson set everything with Sandra - that ended with her trying to kill Bea - into motion. They should charge him as an accomplice in her crimes."

"No! I had nothing to do with her attacking Bea." Law denied before he turned his full attention to my future wife. "I swear, Bea, I love you still. I would never do something like that."

"It seems to me that even you don't know the limits to what you will and won't do to suit your own needs. I thought you leaving me with a breakup note on our wedding day, just moments before I was supposed to walk down the aisle, was bad. You keep proving that your bullshit went so much deeper. I don't even know who the hell you are and I'm ashamed to say I ever dated you, let alone agreed to be married to you."

"No. Don't say that! You don't mean it." Bea's ex pleaded with her.

"Oh, I absolutely mean it. Honestly, my hope is that a little jail time will set you straight and make you realize that the world doesn't revolve around you and your wants alone."

Before he could respond again, the security officers moved out of the way to allow two sheriff's deputies into the room. "Lawson Gregory, you are under arrest for filing false documents with the Clerk of Court."

"You may end up adding to his charges based on what he admitted while our body cams were rolling." One of the guards added helpfully. I gave him a courtesy nod which he returned.

"We'll take this out of the room, so you can recuperate, but we do need to get a statement from you soon, Ms. Robeson."

"She has to get X-rays before she can be discharged, but we can stop by the department afterward, if she's feeling up to it." I offered. Anything that would help keep Sandra behind bars, even if it was a little uncomfortable for Bea, it would be worth it. "Bea will also need a no contact order for both Sandra and Lawson."

"We will let the sheriff and magistrate know to expect that."

"What? Bea is in no danger from me!" Law denied loudly.

"Look at where she is, asshole," I shot back at him. "She's in here because of bullshit you set into motion."

"I didn't think Sandra would hurt her."

"Well, you don't seem to have a whole lot going on in that brain of yours, so I'm not too surprised."

"Fuck you, Ky!"

"You might want to lube up before you're booked, dick-wad!" I hit back. "The boys in prison are going to eat you up with that face."

We watched as the deputies cuffed Lawson, read him his rights, and removed him from the room. "We'll make sure that the authorities get our footage. Take care of yourself, Miss." The security officers left just after the deputies and then the nurse who had come in with Law was the only one who remained behind.

"No offense, honey, but your life sounds a lot like a soap opera."

Bea laughed until she winced. "Yeah, you can say that again."

"Let's get you down for those X-rays. I have a feeling you'll be due for more pain meds by the time you're done." The nurse turned to me after that. "I don't know that she'll be up to giving a statement today because of the drugs they're giving her for pain, but when she does give it, you might want to time it so that she makes the statement just before she's due for more meds. She needs to take them about every four-to-six hours as needed for the first two days and then she can wean down from there."

It took another three hours at the hospital before someone could read the X-rays and decide that Bea didn't have any fractures or breaks in her hip or knee. By then she just wanted to get home and go to sleep, so I sent a message to one of the deputies who had slipped us his card. I let them know they could come to the apartment to speak to her, since she wasn't up to a bunch of traveling around.

In all honesty, they didn't really need her statement, since there was video evidence of everything that happened with Sandra. The rent-a-cops for the hospital also had video of Law's admission. If there was such a thing as justice, Law would serve the full ten years possible for falsifying documents and Sandra would be buried under the fucking courthouse for hurting Bea the way she did.

"I know it isn't possible yet, but the minute they clear up the fraudulent marriage certificate issue, we're getting married again - this time for real. I could have lost you and you would never have legally been my wife. That isn't something I can accept."

My woman offered a tiny smile and then leaned her head to the side. "When we get home, all I want to do is snuggle into your side and listen to your heartbeat. When she came at me in that car, I didn't think I'd ever have that luxury again."

"I think we can arrange that." After I got Bea out to my car, and carefully buckled her in, she closed her eyes and leaned her head against the window. There was no way she could be asleep yet, but I didn't want to bother her with needless conversation. Josh had sent me the video his buddy took of the attempt on Bea's life with the car. He mumbled excuses about why his friend was taking video of Bea walking to begin with, but it was something that I'd over-looked because I was thankful there was evidence of that bitch's double attempt to end my woman's life. If she wasn't in jail, I'd be tempted to return the favor on her, only I wouldn't fuck it up. The bitch would be dead for what she put Bea through. Logically, I knew that Law couldn't have foreseen Sandra's actions, but I still blamed him for his part in trying to keep me and Bea apart, especially since he didn't even seem to want her back then. Then again, he was the asshole who had kept her dangling from a string in the hopes that he would have a backup plan.

"Stupid fucker," I mumbled out loud.

"What?" Bea asked as her head tilted in my direction.

"Nothing, sorry, sweetheart. I'd tell you to get some rest, but we'll be at the house soon."

"What about my medication?"

"They phoned the prescription in, and your mom went to pick it up, along with some supplies, so that you wouldn't have to wait in the car or walk around while you're feeling like crap. Your knee and hip might not have a break in them, but they're still sore and standing on them too long might cause more swelling."

"Thank you for taking care of me." She whispered.

"You never have to thank me for that, sweetheart."

Chapter Eighteen

BEA

TWO WEEKS LATER, I made my way back to the Emergency Room to see Dr. Marcus Bellamy. He had been the one to stitch me up. When I called to see if he was on duty to remove my stitches, I was promptly informed that the doctor would be too busy to handle something as mundane as suture removal. It wasn't like he needed to be the one to do it, I just had a weird thing about follow-up care needing to be done by the same person who did the initial care.

Once I got to the hospital, I was ushered back to the triage room right away. My temperature, weight, and all the answers to the usual intrusive questions were taken before Dr. Bellamy popped his head in after a quick knock.

"Hey, I heard you were back for suture removal. Nurse Harding is going to handle that for you today, but I just wanted to take a quick look at how well everything healed up, if you don't mind."

"That's fine with me." I held my arm out for him to observe. I'd purposely worn a tank top because it was hotter than standing right next to Satan's fire pit. It also helped so that whoever removed my stitches would have easy access to the area without worrying over keeping my sleeves out of their business.

"Looks like everything healed up nicely. Give it a couple more weeks post removal, and you can try using a good scar cream. I'll leave a recommendation in your chart, so you can take that with you when you go. It most likely won't completely eliminate the scar, but it will help to diminish it quicker."

"Thank you, I appreciate that."

It didn't take long to have the stitches removed, and while Nurse Harding was kind and seemed to be capable, it felt incredibly weird to have each strand of the sutures removed from my skin. Then there were the tiny little holes that appeared where the threads were removed. My nurse noticed my scrunched-up face as I glared down at my arm.

"It will all heal up nicely. Those little marks won't even be visible in a couple weeks. The jagged line for the cut will be the worst of it. Dr. Bellamy already put his recommendation for a good cream to help with that, but I will caution you to wait at least two weeks from now. Make sure everything is completely healed before you try to put any of that on your scarring."

"Don't worry, I'm not in the habit of ignoring doctor's orders. Nurse's orders either," I tacked on, which made her smile. "I didn't mean to make it sound as though your thoughts were any less important."

She waved me off. "No worries. The doctor's orders should always supersede the nurse's" She leaned in and whispered the rest, "unless they're wrong." We both chuckled softly so as not to disturb anyone who might be in pain, resting, or grieving elsewhere in the ER.

"Thank you so much for getting all this done for me."

"It's what we're here for." She looked as though she debated on something before she spoke again. "I read in your file what happened and saw the footage on the news after the incident. For what it's worth, I'm so glad that you trusted your instincts and rushed out of the way of the car and ducked when you did to avoid the knife. That must have been so scary."

"I didn't have a chance to be scared," I admitted. "Not in the traditional sense, anyway. I was in fight or flight mode the whole time and it didn't really register what I'd been through until a couple days later."

"If you don't mind me saying, I have a friend who is a therapist for trauma victims. If you have any problems processing on your own, or just need to open up to someone, you should contact him. You can check his credentials, he's on staff here at the hospital as well."

I took the card she offered and read his name aloud. "Dr. Jerry Grace." I grinned up at Nurse Harding. "That's an awesome name for a therapist who has to give people a little grace every day."

"Isn't it just?" She asked with a grin on her face. "I won't push, but you should think about going to see him for a few sessions just to give yourself a bit of grace in working around your feelings, especially since you will have to deal with the trial soon."

I nodded my head and tucked the card away in my purse. "Thank you again. I will give it some thought and maybe schedule an appointment. It's hard to talk about what happened with my fiancé because he wants nothing more than to be able to get justice for what happened to me, and he feels like his hands are tied. I think in Ky's eyes, it feels like he failed me for that reason."

"Dr. Grace would probably make an exception to see him as well."

"I'll let Ky know. Thanks again."

"My pleasure."

I stood and went to check out. I got the order for a good scar cream and headed out to start the rest of my day. Thankfully, the ER is open at all hours, so I was able to swing by before my first shift at the daycare. Suzanne offered to give me more time before I started, considering my injuries, but I refused. It wouldn't be worth going to work there if I had to wait even longer to get started. Then she would be down an employee, and I would be bored at home while I waited for my pride to heal - which seemed to be my most serious injury. Everyone and their mother knew about how Law had ditched me on our wedding day for another woman. How he had hired Sandra to keep Ky's attention off me while he tried to figure out whether he wanted me or the other woman. Unfortunately for Jackie, it also came out that she was the woman he left me for.

While she was quick to offer up the fact that she turned Law down, people still harassed her for being a home-wrecker. I didn't see it that way and gave her a call to let her know that. She admitted that she had feelings for Law until he did what he did. Then, it was as if any growing feelings went right into the garbage because she couldn't get over the fact that he would treat me that way. I understood that well enough. If he would do it to me, what made her any different, if his eyes wandered to the next best thing when it was her turn.

Suzanne leaned in as soon as I got to work so she could inspect my arm. "Well, it doesn't look half bad. Don't let the kids bother you about it. If you need to keep it covered while you're here, it won't bother me one bit."

"It should be fine."

"How is that man of yours handling everything, now that it was all made public?"

"Ky is always my champion. He doesn't take shit from anyone speaking ill of me, which might end up landing him in some hot water one day." We both giggled at that. "He's just angry that there isn't a way to get more justice."

"I heard that Lawson fella took a plea deal that kept him out of prison with time served at the local jail."

I rolled my eyes at that. "Yeah, if you want to count the whole 26 hours he spent in jail as 'time served' then I guess so. He did at least have to pay the maximum fine, but his parents ponied up that $10,000 fine, so it's like he got off Scott-free."

"Rotten. He's going to be even worse of a scoundrel to the next woman who comes along, I bet."

"Maybe." That wasn't something I wanted to let into my thoughts. It wasn't my place to discourage other women from entering a relationship with my ex. They would have to learn on their own, just as I did. They at least had a leg up, since the case was made so public where we lived.

"What about the girl who attacked you?"

"Sandra's day in court is coming, though her lawyers are pushing for diminished mental capacity."

"That girl is crazier than a loon, but not in the way that

she didn't understand what she did was wrong," Suzanne offered her opinion. I smiled and nodded my head.

"Unfortunately, I don't get to have a say in that, but from what the district attorney shared with us, I don't think they'll go easy on her based on mental competency because she passed the test to be able to stand trial already. That goes a long way toward throwing out that kind of defense."

"You know I'm hoping for a lengthy sentence, so she doesn't ever get the chance to bother you again."

"You and me both," I whispered as a parent came in to drop off their child. She did a double take before I slid away and went to stow my stuff in the break room.

Just as I went to turn my cell phone off, and leave it locked up with my things, an incoming text dinged.

> Ky: I hope you have an amazing first day, Sweet Bea. We can celebrate getting free of the itchy stitches and the first day at your new job later when you get home. I'll have dinner ready, so you don't have to worry about it.

> Bea: Thanks, honey. I'm turning my phone off until break time. Can't wait to see you later. I miss you already.

Yep, I rolled my eyes at myself. I had become a sappy, lovesick stranger. It was hard to compare my prior relationship with Law to the one I had with Ky because they were like night and day. I couldn't say there were never any good times with Law, but everything was so different when I had my best friend at my side. I felt loved and appreciated without having to wonder if those things were true. I made sure to give it right back to my man too, even if it did make me sound like a crazy, love-sick fool.

I turned my phone off, put it in my locker, and then made my way to the toddler room where my second favorite age kids were starting to show up for the day. "Hi there, everyone. I'm Ms. Bea."

"Bumble!" One little girl shouted while another, younger child, made a buzzing sound.

"Yes, just like a bumble bee, except I don't sting." I reached out and tickled the girl's ribs before moving to the other child. My heart lit up as they both burst into a fit of giggles. The summer job was just what I needed. Working with kids was more therapy than I could have hoped for.

By the end of the day, my face hurt from smiling so darn much. I loved working with the little ones. They were the best. "Look at that beautiful smile," Ky said in greeting when I walked through the door. "I take it everything went well for your first day?"

"God, I love that age. If it paid more, and offered the same benefits, I would work at a daycare full time with the toddlers."

"Nah. You'd miss your little pre-teens too much."

I poked my lip out in a mock pout and then laughed. "You're probably right. They keep me just as entertained only in a slightly different way."

"Come here," he called, and I slipped my shoes off, dropped my purse on the table near the door, and made my way into the kitchen.

"It smells so good in here. Did you cook or order out?"

"Um, a mix. Your mom brought some stuff over, since she knew it was the first day we were both back to work. I had to reheat it in the oven, because she said the microwave simply would not do."

I laughed at the way he mocked my mother because it sounded just like the tone she would use. Mom hated microwaves. She was convinced that they were the bane of existence and the root of all the world's problems somehow. "Well, whatever she made, I can't wait to dig in. I'm famished."

"How did the suture removal go?" I moved closer to Ky and held my arm out. "Wow, I didn't know the doctors added extra bling when they pulled stitches out."

I laughed as we both glanced down at my arm. "The kids managed to put a bunch of stickers on my arm to make my boo-boo feel better. I kept them from putting the stickers on the scar, but they insisted the magic 'feel betters' were in the stickers and that I needed them." I giggled as Ky grinned down at the mess the kids made of my arm earlier. "I'm paraphrasing, of course."

"I bet you are." He leaned in and kissed my forehead. "Come on, let's eat and then we can go snuggle up in bed."

"Hopefully, we can do more than just snuggle. My stitches are out now, so you don't have an excuse anymore." I cocked a brow up at him in challenge and my man simply grinned at me and then rubbed my belly.

"Sure, sweetheart. Didn't want to make the stitches pull and cause you extra healing time."

I rolled my eyes. "I would have been fine. Why did you rub my belly like that?"

"Hoping it's lucky and we have our own little future toddler terror growing in there."

"I told you it was next to impossible timing."

"Our whole relationship has been next to impossible timing and here we are, Sweet Bea. You, me, and maybe our future spawn."

My smile never wavered as we chatted through dinner and long into the night as Ky made slow, sweet love to me. He needed to be gentle the first time since my accident and I guess there was a part of me that needed that too because it felt as though we grew closer than we ever had been. As I laid there, content and snuggled up to Ky with his heartbeat in my ear, he stroked his fingers through my curls as gently as he could, so he wouldn't catch and pull my hair.

"I'm glad the asshole took a plea." That was not something I expected Ky to say. I glanced up at him and asked, "Why?" He shrugged and continued to play with my hair. "It's bad enough we have to wait for a trial for Sandra. It would have been worse, especially with media coverage, if we had to wait for a separate trial for Law as well."

"Yeah, but he got off without any real consequences."

"Sweetheart, he suffered the worst consequence of all."

"Yeah? How do you figure?"

"He lost you."

Chapter Nineteen

KY

IT TOOK us two months to finally put together a wedding we both wanted. Bea was not pregnant, much to my disappointment, and she convinced me that we needed to wait a bit before we tempted fate and had a baby. She wanted to be officially married before she got pregnant, and she also wanted for us to have a little time together as a couple before we brought a tiny person who would be completely reliant on us into the world. She wasn't wrong. The more she talked about it, the more I saw the validity of her points.

We'd waited so long to be together. It only made sense to enjoy it for a little while. Plus, I wanted us to find a house that would fit a growing family better than my apartment did. My place had three bedrooms, but I used one as an at home office/gym. When we eventually had a baby, we would need a nursery and a guest room for the family I knew would end up crashing at our place to help out during the initial months of having a newborn around. We definitely needed more space for that, maybe even a second floor.

"What are you lost in thought about?" Flynn asked. "It better not be that you've finally come to your senses and decided not to marry my sister."

"Fuck no! That thought never crossed my mind." Flynn grinned at me as I offered up my denial.

"No hesitation. I like it. Always knew you'd be good with Bea."

"Thanks. I was thinking about how we needed a bigger place before we have a baby."

"Is she pregnant?"

"Not yet," I told him as I smirked his way. "But we won't have too much time alone, if I can help it."

"Jesus. I don't need to hear about how you're planning to knock up my sister."

I shrugged my shoulders and turned back to the mirror to adjust my tie. "She is the woman of my dreams. One day, when you find yours, you'll understand."

"Already found the woman of my dreams and she chose to be with someone else because she knew him longer."

I cocked my head to the side and thought about who he could mean. "You talking about Beckett's fiancé?" I asked.

"She only saw Beckett. I only saw her. He... Well, fuck knows what Beckett saw back then, but I've noticed his eyes aren't only for her anymore."

"You can't interfere in that. It won't end in your favor if you do."

"Know that." Flynn grumbled. "Let's get you down there before people start to worry."

"I'm not the one they need to worry about."

"My sister sure the fuck isn't going to get cold feet. I found one of her diaries when she was younger, and swear to God, she had her name and your last name written together on every other page. Bea has always wanted to marry you."

I chuckled. "She may have mentioned her habit of signing my name back in the day. I think it's cute. We each always knew we should end up together." I clapped him on his back. "Maybe, things will work out for you too. If you've noticed Beckett's eyes wandering, chances are Courtney has noticed as well."

"Yeah, but even if she does, I'm probably the last person she would look at to have a potential future with. I'm the asshole's cousin. She'll probably think we're two rotten apples from the same tree."

"As long as the tree has branches, I think you're good," I joked.

"Shut up, asshole, before I lock you in the basement and sabotage your wedding day."

"Nuh-uh. Nothing is messing with this day. We have already dotted all our Ts and crossed our Is."

"I think you got that backward, dickhead."

"Whatever," I called out to him as he ran over to open the door to his parent's backyard. "Wow!" I came up behind him and took in the spectacle. The Robeson women had gone all out to make sure mine and Bea's day went off without a hitch, including the way they turned the backyard into a fantasyland. There were twinkling lights somehow strung up overhead that led all the way to a pergola that was draped in white tulips and some sort of tiny yellow flowers with green vines. Whatever they were, they smelled really sweet.

"She's going to love this," I mentioned as I took in the

way the chairs were arranged on either side of the lit-up walkway. There was a white runner carpet down on the ground that led to the altar we created on the other side of the pergola where the two of us would stand to take our vows.

Flynn and I got into place, since he was my best man. Once we were in place, Bea's mom called for everyone to take their seats. We only had close friends and family there for the event. There were less than fifty people, but it felt like our whole world was in attendance as I stood there and waited for the one person among them who I couldn't live without. Mina made her way down the aisle first and stood at the end on the bride's side as Bea's maid of honor. Then the music shifted, and Bea and her dad marched down the aisle toward me. She wore a gorgeous, fitted dress that hugged her curves and made my mouth water. It looked like a silky material and boasted spaghetti straps and a bit of lace and beading detail that made the bodice stand out a bit more. She opted to come down the aisle barefoot since we were doing an at-home wedding.

As soon as her dad placed her hand in mind, I pulled my soon-to-be-wife - for real this time - into my space and kissed her lips.

"Son, we haven't gotten to that part yet," the pastor we hired to officiate stated. Our audience laughed along with him, but I refused to give my woman once I had her in my arms. I kept her locked in close to me as we each recited our vows. My arm stayed wrapped around her waist until it was time to place rings on our fingers. Then, and only then, did I release my grip on her. It wasn't that I thought she was going to run. It was more like I had to touch her to make it all real. We were finally here. Finally saying "I do" for real.

"I will love you with every bit of my heart from now until I take my last breath," I promised along with my "I do."

"I will also love you with every bit of my heart from now until I take my last breath," she repeated as she placed my ring back on my finger. I'd never taken it off while we waited for everything to be fixed, so that Bea was legally able to marry someone who wasn't Lawson Gregory - the fucking prick.

"This is the part where you get to kiss the bride," the pastor leaned forward and whisper-yelled it as if we were in cahoots. I ignored him, the laughter of everyone gathered to watch us become man and wife, and I took my woman in a smoldering kiss that promised things would only get more heated later on when we were able to spend our first night together as husband and wife - for real.

"I'd marry you again, if you asked me tomorrow," Bea whispered in my ear as everyone we knew and loved cheered our new union.

"Maybe I'll do just that."

Epilogue

"DADDY, why do you and Momma have two different wedding anniversaries?"

"Did you ask your mom?" I stared at my oldest daughter, who turned fourteen a few days ago, as she shook her head. "Why not?"

"She was busy with Kinnie." I chuckled and wondered what my 7-year-old had gotten up to that kept my wife so busy. Kincaid was our youngest, the only boy of the bunch, and he kept us on our toes like the girls never did.

"Well," I saw movement from around the corner and rolled my eyes. The little asshole, who was my daughter's best friend, didn't need to hear this story. He'd get bigger ideas about my Lina than I wanted him to have. "Get over here Colton. No point in hiding when I already saw you."

The boy, to his credit, marched into the room with his shoulders back and head held high, as if he hadn't just been caught sneaking around. Lina grinned at Colton as he rolled his eyes at her. The slight pink of his cheeks told me I was on the money with my original assessment. The little shit had it bad for my daughter. I wondered if it was how I used to come across to Bea's dad when we were younger. Not that it mattered. One thing I knew for certain was that Bea's parents never interfered with our friendship and I couldn't do the same with Lina and Colt.

"Take a seat, this is a bit of a long story."

They sat so close their bodies touched from shoulders to hips, hips to knees and down to their feet. A low growl of disapproval escaped, and Colt had enough sense to slide over an inch or two while my daughter poked her lip out in an unhappy pout.

"Bea and I were childhood friends."

"Did you ever date when you were in school?" Colt asked before I could even get the story started. Yep, the bastard had it bad for my girl. I shook my head in answer. That wasn't good enough for him though as he followed up with another quick question. "Why not? You ended up married eventually, so you must have liked her back then."

"I did like her back then and she liked me too. We just didn't know the other felt that way. Every time one of us got up the nerve to take our friendship further, the other had given up for different reasons and decided we were better off friends." I chuckled. "Bea and I kept missing telling each other how we felt by minutes sometimes. That's what happened when she met the first man she was engaged to."

Lina gasped. "Mom was engaged? Before you?" She added on to clarify.

"Yep. It was another one of those times I had finally got the nerve to tell her exactly how I felt about her. I even asked her out on a date, though she didn't know that was what it was at the time."

"Then what happened?" Colt asked.

"Bea had some car trouble. The two men that stopped for her were Law and Todd. They were best friends, and Todd was really interested in Bea. He was the one to make his friend stop to help her when Law would have just passed right by. Once the idiot got a good look at your mom, he decided to ask her out and she agreed."

"Wait, but you had a date set up."

"We did. In my mind it was a date. In Bea's mind, it was just dinner. When she told me all about the knight in shining armor who rescued her, and how he asked her out on a date for the next night, I knew I'd waited too long again. She missed our dinner date because of being broken down and she had already accepted a date for the next night with someone else."

"Aw, man! That sucks, dude."

"It really does," I agreed with Colt.

"Why didn't you tell her that your dinner was supposed to be a date?" My daughter asked.

"She seemed so damn happy about it." I shrugged my shoulders. "Even if I couldn't have the woman I wanted, my biggest wish was always for your mom to be happy. So, I let her go and hoped the guy was an asshole or something, so I could get my shot again."

"That obviously didn't happen, since they got engaged," Lina mumbled.

"Did you forget your parents are married?" Colt teased her and bumped her shoulder.

"Yeah, but she almost married someone else."

"She did," I agreed.

"So, he wasn't an asshole?" Colt asked.

I laughed. "Oh, no. He was a major asshole and he proved it by leaving Bea a note on their wedding day telling her that he was going to shoot his shot with another woman whom he had been falling for. She was someone he worked with. That woman turned him down because he was the kind of asshole who would leave his bride at the church on her wedding day."

"At least she was smart," Lina huffed.

"Yep, but so was I. When your mom told me what happened, I told her to meet me down the aisle and that her wedding day wouldn't be wasted."

Lina squealed as Colt nodded his head knowingly.

"So, you got married."

"Yes and no. This is where the two anniversaries come into play." I told the kids about how our first marriage wasn't legal and we had to wait to get married for real, but the minute we were able to, I married Bea all over again.

"Wow! That's so romantic. I'm so glad Law was an asshole."

"Language," I growled at my daughter.

"You let Colton say it like twice now."

"Colt isn't my kid, you are. You're right though. We're all very happy that Law was a stupid asshole who didn't realize he had the best woman in the world by his side, ready to marry him."

"So, what happened to that guy?"

"He ended up in jail for about a day for fraud and had to pay a $10,000 fine. He landed on his feet eventually thanks to his rich parents who bailed him out and paid the fine. That didn't stop his employer from firing him for having a fraud conviction on his record, though." I didn't need to tell them about Sandra's part in everything or how she was found guilty on two attempted homicide charges as well as assault with a deadly weapon. She was still in prison serving out her forty-year sentence.

"Did he ever get married?" My sweet daughter asked.

"Pretty sure he's been married four or five times now."

"So, he never learned his lesson, huh?"

"Nope. Some people are just terminally stupid from birth."

"That's never going to be us," Lina suggested as she reached over and took Colt's hand. Her best friend grinned at her.

"Nope. We're gonna get married and have lots of babies together."

"What the fuck? Bea!" I yelled for my wife because she was going to need to help me dig a hole out back to bury the little shit in.

"What?" Bea ran in exasperated with Kinnie hot on her heels.

"They're talking about getting married and having babies. Get the shovel."

"Oh that?" My wife asked, as if she already knew their plans. I narrowed my eyes on Bea and she giggled. While it was cute as fuck, I didn't think the situation warranted giggles.

"They're 14."

"Yep, and I think they already had at least two fake weddings.

"Wait, what? How do you know?"

"I was there for them," Bea announced.

I turned back to my daughter. "You had two fake weddings and didn't ask me to walk you down the aisle?"

"Sorry, Dad. I thought you'd freak out."

"I will. I don't care if it's a fake wedding when you're 12 or a real one when you're 42. I will absolutely freak out, but I still want to be there to walk you down that aisle. You're my baby. You need to know that even if I do, one day when you're like 53, give you away to the man of your dreams, I will always be there to pick you up if you fall down - or if he screws up." I turned my gaze on Colt as I said the last bit.

"Aww, Dad," Lina mumbled as she threw herself into my arms. "I love you. I'm definitely getting married way sooner than 42 or 53 though. That's really old. Like, I don't think I could even have babies when I get that old."

My wife rolled her eyes at our daughter. "You might want to keep the 'old stuff' down a bit, your mom is getting offended." Bea rolled her eyes at me again and then blew me a kiss before going back to whatever mess she had to clean up with our youngest terror.

"No more getting married without me, promise?"

"I promise."

"Good. Now, I think it's time Colton went home and thought about the fact that if he ever hurts my beautiful baby girl, I will dig a hole in the backyard and bury him in it. Then I'll plant an endangered species on top of it so no one can ever dig up his body."

"Dad!"

"I'd never hurt my future wife," Colt tossed out coolly until I stood up and tossed my daughter onto the couch, so I could go after the smug little shit.

"Bye Mrs. Armstrong."

"Better run fast, Colton!" Bea called back to him. I heard the door close and then turned to see my daughter grinning so big it looked like her face might actually stick like that.

"What are you so happy about?"

"I'm really going to marry that boy one day, Dad." It was my turn to pout. "Don't worry, I wouldn't want anyone else to walk me into my future, except you." Lina got up and ran off as my wife came back into the room without our son in tow.

"Have I told you lately how much I love you?"

I shook my head and pulled my beautiful wife into my arms. She locked her hands around my neck and smiled up at me with those plump lips of hers. I brushed some of her stray curls back out of her face and wouldn't even think of pointing out how a couple of them had a silver sheen. She was still just as beautiful as when we married and even more so than when I had fallen in love with her long before that. She was the mother to my three children, the woman of my dreams, and I got to love her up every chance I got. I never admitted it to anyone, but I thanked Law every night, when I laid down beside my woman, that he was too stupid to see the treasure he tossed aside.

"I love you even more now than I ever have before," She told me.

"Is that right?" I asked

"Yup. You were so sweet with them just now even though I know it killed you to admit that your daughter is of an age where she is considering who she might marry one day."

"We still have a few years to go before she can do anything about that legally. I have time to plot and plan."

Bea giggled again and the sound was music to my ears. I leaned in closer and breathed her in. She smelled like cupcakes thanks to the mess she and our son made in the kitchen. "You have time but you won't do anything to impede her happiness and that is why you are the very best man this world has to offer."

"Yeah?"

"Definitely. Pretty sure I should reward you for being such a good man later on tonight."

"I'm not going to turn down your rewards, Sweet Bea. I love you more than I did the first time I fell in love with you."

She smiled at me again as I leaned in and kissed her lips. "Just how many times have you fallen in love with me, Ky?"

"At least once a day since we met."

"We met when we were kids," she reminded me needlessly.

"Yeah, and I've been falling more in love with you every day since then."

"You are the very best man! Let's hope, for our daughter's sake, that Colt follows in your footsteps." Bea winked at me as she walked away. "Don't forget to meet me upstairs around ten for your reward, handsome."

I truly was the luckiest man alive.

Thank you for reading

WHEN THE LAST PETAL FALLS BY CHRISTINE MICHELLE

For new release news, updates, book recommendations, bonus content, and ARC opportunities, sign up for my newsletter:
https://christineandanne.myflodesk.com/newsletter

If you enjoyed this series, you should read:

A Different Husband

Christine Michelle

COURTNEY

I always thought Beckett was the man who I would marry. He had been my everything since we were 10. We were engaged by the time I turned 22.

Then, one day, he came to me with a plan to help save his

cousin's inheritance. It would make me the villain of the story in everyone else's eyes. It would also mean that walk down the aisle would happen with the wrong man.

Still, Beckett asked. I granted him this crazy scheme, played along, and quickly learned that he had agreed to it because it freed him from me for a little while. I never knew he wanted out. He never let on until I had a different husband's ring on my finger and was forced to watch from the sidelines as Beckett carried on with other women.

Flynn was the shoulder I leaned on, and we grew closer as a result. Eventually, Beckett began to notice me again, but somewhere along the line, things changed. When I saw my future, he was no longer the man wearing the ring that matched my own.

FLYNN

My cousin won our mutual best friend's heart long ago.
I'd hated him for it then.
I hated him for allowing her to marry me 'temporarily' even more.

I'd always been a little in love with Courtney, but watching as the light left her eyes when her fiancé threw her away and paraded other women in front of her made me want to show my beautiful new wife what it was like to be with the right Robeson man. I wanted to bring her light back. The only problem was, I had to do it before my cousin realized just how badly he had screwed up by letting her go in the first place.

A Different Husband is the third book in the Robeson Family Novels, but it is a standalone story. The Robeson Family Novels can be read in any order. There is no cheating by main characters in this book, despite the arranged marriage.

Chapter 1

Courtney

"I need you to marry Flynn instead of me at our wedding."

My fiancé's words didn't register because I was too concerned with the fact that my mother wanted me to use silver and purple as our wedding colors. They had been our elementary and high school colors, and she thought it would be adorable that we marched into the future while paying homage to the roots of our love story. In theory, it sounded great, but my eyes continued to dart back to the pictures of the beautiful peach floral arrangements that were sent to me last week.

My wedding was only a few weeks away and everything needed to be finalized. The flowers and cake were the final items, and they were only still on the to-do list because I couldn't pick a complementary color. Silver was a given. Peach was my choice, purple my mother's. I continued to stare at the peach floral arrangement as I tried to wrap my head around what Beckett had just asked of me.

"I'm sorry, you need me to do what?" I asked the question as I blinked rapidly in an attempt to unsee the man standing before me, considering he had just asked me to do the unthinkable.

Beckett Robeson, the man I'd been a little bit in love with since all the way back in elementary school, did not change what he said, nor did what I thought was a waking nightmare end. Instead, he grinned down at me as he took my hands into his own and made me a stupid promise.

"Everything will be fine. Flynn just needs to know that it's someone the family can trust. I promise, all of this," he offered as he let go of my hand with one of his in order to sweep over the wedding plans I'd meticulously crafted – *our* wedding plans – "can wait until after we help Flynn."

"Beckett?" I questioned, but he continued to grin at me like a complete freaking idiot. His slightly wavy hair had come free of the gel he used to slick it back. As it flopped down into his eyes again, I realized just how nervous he must have been for the conversation. He only ever pushed his hands through his hair when his nerves got the best of him. Still, I couldn't fathom him ever getting himself worked up about this particular issue. My fiancé wanted me to marry his cousin instead. Even if it was a temporary arrangement, how could he even suggest that?

"You can't be serious."

My fiancé sat down beside me, and once again took both of my hands in his. I wanted him to appear forlorn over this situation, or at the very least, a bit put out by the demands of his family. Instead, there was an excited gleam in his eyes that looked a lot like giddiness. The man who was supposed to love me forever shouldn't seem triumphant about asking me to marry someone else.

"Courtney, you have to understand, it's not just about what Flynn stands to gain. Hell, the crazy bastard was willing to give it all up. The problem is that his family's business is also on the chopping block if he doesn't settle the terms of our grandfather's Last Will and Testament. I told you that Grandfather didn't include me as the backup. I can't inherit any of it. I don't think Flynn knows that either, or at least he hasn't realized yet. This way, maybe I can get him to sell me the cabin. You know what it means to me."

"I understand all that, Beckett. What I don't understand is why I have to be *that* person. We were planning our own wedding." I pulled my hand free from his and lifted the pictures of table settings I'd been going through. "These were supposed to be for us, *our* memories. This was *MY* dream wedding." My voice took on a pleading tone as I stared into his caramel-colored eyes and practically begged him to change his mind and not ask this of me. When he said nothing, I continued. "*Our* wedding! *Our* memories! Doesn't that mean anything to you?"

"Sweetheart, I know you've worked hard on this, but that's also what makes it perfect. All the details are already set. All you have to do is show up and say your vows to my cousin instead of me."

He shrugged his shoulders as if it really weren't that big of a deal. Instead of him being my one and only by the time we got married, I would be divorced from someone else if I went along with this crazy plan to marry his cousin. It made my heart ache just to think of it. Beckett had truly been my one and only. He was my first everything and I was his. I couldn't imagine saying, 'I do' to anyone else, for any reason.

"But then my dream wedding and all this planning will be for someone else. Then what am I supposed to do for our wedding?"

Once again, my eyes tracked the up and down motion of his shoulders. The indifferent gesture killed something deep down inside of me. If I had to put a finger on what that thing was that died, I'd say it was my hope. The twinkle in his eyes made Beckett seem younger than his 25 years somehow. We had been middle school sweethearts, though I'd loved him long before that. We continued our relationship all through high school. I waited to be married to him until he had his MBA, just as we planned. This was finally supposed to be our time to make everything as official as it could be. So, why did my fiancé seem happy to hand me off to his cousin instead?

"What does Flynn have to say about all this?"

Beckett chuckled. "Flynn didn't think I'd be able to convince you to do it."

The three of us had grown up together, gone to school together, and had known one another since Flynn was pulled out of his stuffy private academy in middle school. After moving to slum it with the rest of us in public school, Beckett's cousin had become a third wheel whenever we would hang out. I knew Flynn and liked him just fine. He had even been one of my best friends for the longest time, but he wasn't the boy I always dreamed of marrying. He knew me well enough to know that I wouldn't want any part of this, so why didn't my own fiancé know the same thing?

"What if I said 'no'?" The determined look in Beckett's eyes said everything I needed to know. He would be angry with me if I didn't go along with this scheme.

"Come on, Sweetheart. It's not forever."

"It is a legally binding marriage, Beckett!"

"Meh!" He made the noise in an exaggerated, exasper-ated way that grated on my nerves. "Courtney, do this for me, for us, for our future children."

"What are you going on about? Why would this be good for our future children?"

My fiancé rolled his eyes at me again, as if I should already know the answer. "Flynn plans on compensating you for your time and trouble."

I gasped. "This is about money?" I had gone to school to be an art teacher. What I really wanted to do was to one day become a successful artist in my own right, but until that day, I could teach other children out there who had a passion for the arts the way that I had been taught when I was in school. Granted, it didn't pay that well, but Beckett had his MBA. He worked for an amazing firm out of Atlanta and made a solid six figure income. We didn't need anything else.

"No, not really. It's just that we have plenty to be comfortable, but…" His words trailed off. His eyes pleaded with me to understand.

"But what?"

"But this could set us up for retirement, our children's education, you would never have to teach. You could just stay home and paint and not have to worry about whether your work will ever sell or not."

"Beckett," I whispered his name as my heart cracked wide open. "This is not okay."

"Please, Courtney. Do this for me. Do it for Flynn and his family. When it's all over, we'll have our day, and our future will be set financially so that we never have to worry about anything."

"Fine." I agreed reluctantly. If my own fiancé wasn't going to fight against this stupid plan, then why should I?

"I make plenty, but I'm already worried how we'll afford college for the three children you want to have," his argument continued when the one word I said didn't sink in right away.

"I said, *fine!*" I reiterated with a little snap in my tone.

"You – what? Oh! Shit, I didn't realize. Seriously? You'll do it?" Every word out of his mouth was said in rapid-fire succession, as if he needed to hurry before I changed my mind.

"I hope you don't regret asking me to do this." The warning sat hot on my tongue, because I already knew this would do more than put a few cracks in the shiny veneer of our relationship. This would eventually destroy us. I felt it in my bones. It was too bad that Beckett didn't seem to realize, or maybe it was just that he truly didn't care.

Also by Christine Michelle

CHRISTINE MICHELLE

Robeson Family Novels (standalones)

The Forgotten Wife · When the Last Petal Falls · A Different Husband

Standalone Novels

The Groupie Journal

Letters to Lily

His Bittersweet Regret

Bad at Love

TFO

The Fortunate Ones

T.I.E. Series

The Infinite Something · The Infinite Beat

Valhalla Rising

Revived

Kings of Anarchy MC: New Mexico

Property of Bigfoot

Aces High MC – Dakotas

Dancing with Danger · Whiskey Tango Foxtrot · The Restart and the Remedy

Aces High MC – Charleston

The Other Princess · A Love So Hard · The Princess and the Prospect · The Killing Ride · A Twist of Fate · Everlasting · A Year and a Day ·The Broken Beginning – Part One ·The Broken Beginning – Part Two

Aces High MC – Tallahassee

Crushed

Aces High MC – Sierra High

Walker

Aces High MC – Cedar Falls

Redemption Weather · Proven · Smoke and the Flame · Redemption Duology Box Set

S.H.E. MC

Angel Girl · JoJo · Keys

Dark Leopards MC (paranormal)

Ridden by Darkness · The B Team

Mirage Island Mates

Into the Grasslands

Seasons Pack Series

Winter Wolves

The Ancients Series

Shadows of the Ancients · Falling into the White · Branches of the Willow · Bound by the Moon

Vukodlak Brew Series

Entwined · Enraged

The Awakening Series

Birthrights · Revelations · Incarnations

Death Viewers

Breathless

Upper YA Titles

The Voodoo Follies

Catch a Falling Star

ANNE STORM

Savage Vipers MC

Loved for the Holidays

Cheating Hearts Series

About the Author

Christine Michelle (also known as: Anne Storm) runs on coffee and giggles as she writes her angst-fueled romance stories (motorcycle club, rockstar, paranormal, college, & other contemporary as well as women's fiction and marriage in trouble novels).

She is a mom to four humans (2 girls, 2 boys – all grown now).

When she's not writing books, she enjoys reading, drawing, hiking, or feeding her soul with live music at concerts.

Christine is a traveler and has lived all over the USA (and other parts of the world). She currently lives in Rapid City, South Dakota with her two fur babies.

Buy direct from me:

https://christineandanne.com/

Sign up for my newsletter:

https://christineandanne.myflodesk.com/newsletter

Universal social links:

https://linktr.ee/christinemichelle

facebook.com/M00nlitDreams

instagram.com/christinemichelle_annestorm

tiktok.com/@christine.michelle.books

www.ingramcontent.com/pod-product-compliance
Lightning Source LLC
Chambersburg PA
CBHW020648260626
47157CB00008B/2951